BIGFOOT of YONAH RIDGE

by
BILLY PLANT III

Bigfoot of Yonah Ridge

Copyright © 2020 by Billy Plant III

ISBN-13: 978-0-9915818-3-2

www.mazedog.com

This is a work of fiction. Any characters resembling actual persons, living or dead, is purely coincidental.

The most developed science remains a continual becoming.
-Jean Piaget

Author's Note

While many of the locations and geologic formations in this novel are actual places, I have taken artistic liberties with distances and spatial relationships, as well as zoology and some animal physiology.

Once upon a time...

Chapter 1

The October sky arched cobalt blue over the Earth, late afternoon, no clouds. A hawk glided circles on rising currents of air. Far below, through the forest canopy of turning leaves, Henry Davidson sheathed his machete, shouldered his surveying rod, turned, and began walking through a mature woodland of yellow-leaved oak, hickory, and beech. The dry autumn air and crisp fallen leaves that crunched beneath his boots sent up a sharp, burnt odor with each step. Thirty-one years old, six-foot-one, and wearing a full beard and a thick mane of dark brown hair tucked under a ball cap, Henry was just one more surveyor in the long line of surveyors who had been pacing and pulling chains across these same hills and hollows for over two hundred years, measuring the land, recording the limits of where one man's claim to what is rightfully God's alone ended and another's began. He pushed his way through an underbrush of mountain laurel and tangles of grape vines, peering ahead, looking for an open spot where he would set the next traverse point.

After two hundred feet he broke into a small clearing on the ridge. A deer lay dead on the rocky soil. The deer's eye was still opaque, but stared the thousand-yard, vacant stare that sees nothing. There was no stench of death, but flies had already begun to swarm about the dead animal's orifices. Henry nudged the animal's velvety ten-point rack with the tip of his surveying rod. "Nice deer. Hasn't been dead very long," he thought. There were no external signs of trauma and Henry estimated that the deer weighed about 130 pounds so it had obviously not starved to death. He had run across two other such deer during the summer and at one point contacted a Tennessee Wildlife Resources officer to report them and ask what had been causing the deer to die. The TWRA officer had told him about the Epizootic Hemorrhagic

Disease (EHD), a virus that had been spreading through deer populations and had been exacerbated by the summer's prolonged drought. He imagined that this deer was yet another victim.

Despite the deer and the potential for a rotting carcass if they had to return to this site before the boundary was finished, Henry decided this clearing would be an ideal place to set the next traverse point. "Can you see me, Skip?" he called out to the man running the instrument (I-man) who had by this time walked up to the point Henry had just occupied. "I'm waving the rod up high," he continued, lifting the surveying rod up above his head and swaying it from side to side.

"Yeah, I see you. But not down low. We're gonna have to chop out the line," replied Skip Reeves in a gravelly voice, gargley wet from years of cigarette smoke. With grizzled jowls and a time-worn face, Skip was a veteran I-man with countless boundaries all over middle Tennessee under his belt.

"That's fine. You'll like this set up. Its right beside a big dead buck," yelled Henry.

"Another dead deer? This one don't stink does it?"

"No. It looks like it just died a few hours ago."

Henry pulled out his machete and began chopping out a clear line of sight back toward where the I-man was setting up. The third man, who ran the backsight rod (think of it as measuring something you already know the distance of as a way checking the precision of your surveying instrument) came up to chop as well.

"Its hotter 'n hell out here for October," said Skip. "My ol' lady thinks I'm out working half days and partying all night with all our per diem but she would be wrong. I'm sweatin' my ass off out here," he said, flailing his machete through the brush.

"It's hot. But the weather is gonna break before too long. It's mid-October," said Eddy Allen, aspiring musician and off-and-on survey tech in between paying gigs as a bass player in a rock-n-roll cover band.

After ten minutes a clear line of sight had been chopped through the underbrush. Skip and Eddy walked back to their respective stations. Henry returned to the clearing and drove a wooden hub into the forest floor, twenty feet away from the deer carcass. When everyone was situated Henry held the surveying rod plumb on a metal tack in the hub. "Okay, I'm good," he shouted, keeping his eye on the leveling bubble mounted on the rod.

"I'm lookin'" shouted Skip, then, after gaining perfect alignment on the rod and sending forth the laser to read the distance and angle of the prism on top, Skip shouted "Good!"

"Come ahead!" yelled Henry. He picked up his bag, shouldered the rod, and walked ahead, repeating the process as they had done dozens of times, steadily making their way around the one-thousand-acre tract that in a few months would hypothetically be subjected to the dynamite, track hoes and bulldozers of land developers.

The tract of land Henry and his crew were surveying was bordered on one side by the Calfkiller River in Lytle County, Tennessee, some eighty miles southeast of Nashville. The whole area is a landscape of steep hills and narrow hollows and gorges where the sun only penetrates at the apex of its arc across the sky. High ridges, like the one they were traversing, gave way to steep slopes, honeycombed with caves and dripping with springs, cascades, and waterfalls. The land was wild and undeveloped. And, though the forest had been cleared multiple times in the last 180 years, it had recovered and the mature stands of hardwoods tempted loggers to come in to harvest another crop. But timber land is cheap and this long-forgotten tract had attracted the attention of Buddy MacFarland, a developer who had plans to build a complex of retail outlet stores in this remote, economically impoverished mountain community.

Being on travel calls for long days, so at six o'clock, with the golden sun of autumn shining at a bright but low angle on the ridge, Henry walked forward to set one last point for the day. After consulting the property deeds, he left the ridge top and began chopping his way through the underbrush down a steep ravine. He worried that setting a good point would be difficult as the shadows grew ever deeper in the hollow. But this is where the property line broke and, tired from an eleven-hour day in the field, Henry could think of no other option.

As he chopped his way down into the gorge, Henry was overcome by the feeling that he was being watched. He stopped chopping. Descending darkness plays with the nerves of even those accustomed to being out in the wild. "I think I've disturbed some scavenger's evening meal," thought Henry with an amused, nervous smile. His feeling of being watched was verified by a smell which now drifted on the air. The odor of rich forest floor, evergreen boughs, and animal fur, mingled together in a way that was startling but not offensive. He turned toward odor and the imagined eyes, perhaps expecting see a coyote. Instead, he saw a human figure, halfway submerged in the shadows in a tangle of mountain laurel thirty feet away. Whoever, whatever it was, stood motionless. Fully facing the figure, Henry could see that what stood before him was no human at all. It looked to be nearly seven feet tall and covered with reddish-brown hair. What Henry found most disconcerting was the heavy brow and expressive, face which stared an intense gaze from deep-set, darkly calm but piercing eyes.

Henry screamed, a primal instinct of a sound, evolved to call for help in a way that needed no explanation. He dropped his rod and machete, yielding himself defenseless. He stumbled over a small tree, falling clumsily into the underbrush. The creature issued an odd whistling sound, then turned and quietly walked away, deeper into the hollow, quickly becoming lost in the shadows.

After a few stupefied seconds in the paralytic daze of fear, Henry could hear Skip and Eddy's frantic voices calling to him from the ridge above. "Henry? Henry? What the hell just happened? Where are you? Where are you?"

"I'm down here," yelled Henry in a broken voice.

"Are you okay? What th' hell made you scream so?" yelled Skip, genuinely concerned.

Henry stood there, knees weak, hands trembling. When Skip and Eddy got to him, they found him lost in a mental fog. For a minute Henry was quiet, then finally he said, "Let's get out of here. We'll finish up tomorrow."

"I like that idea," said Skip. "It's been a helluva long day. But you still gotta tell us what happened."

"Yeah, what the hell was that all about?" asked Eddy.

"Well, ya'll aren't gonna believe this, but I just saw something really, really weird," answered Henry, sighing, exhaling the fearful tension that gives way to exhaustion.

Chapter 2

French botanist Andre Michaux passed through what is now Lytle County during his 1795 plant collecting expedition. H was so struck with the size of the poplar trees he saw that he referred to the area as Grands Arbres (Tall Trees). The name stuck, anglicizing to Grand Arbor then Frenchifying again and contracting to Arborville, smallest county seat in the state of Tennessee. Lytle County's economic destiny looked dim, like many small Tennessee counties. A few years before, the area lost its largest employer when the Spingwater Paper Company shut down the sawmill. Since the small hospital closed, medical care was over forty-five minutes away. As were the jobs. People who stayed in Lytle County wound up driving to surrounding counties to work in construction, automobile manufacturing, health care. Others made a living from the rocky soil and dense forests, raising livestock or logging, the virgin poplars that inspired Michaux being long gone except for a couple of isolated stands in deep, hidden coves.

At the end of another long hot day spent among all those trees Henry, Skip, and Eddy were ready for something to eat.

The Ridgeline Bar & Grill isn't the only restaurant in Arborville but it is the best one. It sits a at the edge of town, half a mile from the courthouse. A dozen years ago it was featured on a local public television show out of Nashville, the kind of show that features people who carve wood sculptures with chainsaws and any restaurant that smokes meat or bakes a great pie. The Ridgeline was adept at both. Anyone who wanted a good hand-patted cheeseburger or a smoked quarter of chicken with turnip greens and macaroni and cheese on the side could find it here. With its gravel parking lot and decor of taxidermed animals and autographed photos of minor country music stars hanging on the wall, it could never be confused with the slick chain bar and grill establishments that dominate American interstate exits.

Over the course of the week the Ridgeline had become the beacon of light at the end of long days for Henry, Skip, and Eddy. In that time the two waitresses working the dinner shift had gotten to recognize them as they walked in the door. "Hey, ya'll are still here," said Tracy, their favorite server. Fortyish and attractive in a faded-blue-jean-kind-of-way, she smiled then walked briskly to the back to refill a pitcher of sweet tea. The trio sat down at a table. Tracy walked up to the table, setting down three glasses of water. "It's been so hot. Ya'll must've burnt up out there today," she said as she passed the glasses around. "Look, I remembered to put the lemon in your water," she said to Henry.

"Thank you," he replied.

"Tonight's specials are up on the board. You've got your choice between meatloaf and smoked chicken. Randy used a new rub on it this time. It's really good. I'll give ya'll a couple of minutes to decide." As she walked off in her well-fitting faded jeans Skip spoke up.

"I could watch her walk away all day." Henry and Eddy grunted in agreement. "So, you say you saw a bigfoot this evening? What I wanna know is where were you hiding that flask all day?"

"Sounds to me more like that medical marijuana that would stick to the wall," said Eddy, getting in on the ribbing.

"I tell you what I saw was real," said Henry patiently. He understood that there was no reason for anyone to believe that he had seen a large hominid in the woods. A creature celebrated in popular culture but unknown to science.

"Did you tell Richard about it this evening when you called to tell him what we got done?" asked Skip, referring to Richard Cummings, the owner of RC Land Surveying, the company for which they worked.

"No. I didn't want to deal with the hassle of trying to explain it over the phone. I just told him that we had about half a day's work left and we'd be back to Nashville by tomorrow afternoon.

"Thank goodness. I'm about ready to get back and see my ol' lady. That good lookin' waitress is starting to tempt me," said Skip. "Eddy, you ever hook up with any waitress like that out on the road?"

"Well," said Eddy, somewhat coyly. "Yeah, but I'm twenty-four so they are generally younger than her."

At this point Tracy came back to the table to take their order. "All right. Ya'll decided what you'll be having?"

"I'll have the meatloaf, mashed potatoes and fried apples," said Skip. Eddy ordered a cheeseburger and a Coke.

"I'll have the chicken and coleslaw and field peas," said Henry.

"Well it's good to see that your encounter today hasn't affected your appetite," said Skip. Henry looked down and turned his head, ready for what was coming. "Henry here said he saw a bigfoot out in the woods this evening right as we were finishing up."

"A bigfoot?" exclaimed Tracy, incredulous. "They law'. I always knew there was no tellin' what you'd find out there on Yonah Ridge. It's the wildest part of the county. And this is a pretty wild county. I bet you saw a bear. You know that's what *yonah* means? Its Cherokee for bear."

"I didn't know that. It very well could have been," said Henry, wanting to drop the subject.

"Funny thing is, my uncle said he saw a big ape up there once when he was out hunting," said Tracy. "But he drank a lot when he was hunting. He told us that ape story one time but for some reason after that if anybody asked about it, he just told 'em he'd seen a bear standing on its hind legs. But he'd get so drunk out there at his little hunting cabin. I think to his dying day he still believes he saw an ape. But we do have bears around here," she said. "They're coming down from Big South Fork."

"What surprises me is that we haven't seen anyone's marijuana patch," said Eddy, with a distinct hint of disappointment in his voice.

"Well, it's up there. But if you do run across some you best just keep going," advised Tracy. "People get mean when you know they're up to something like that," she said, ripping the order ticket from the writing pad. "I'll go put in this order for ya'll. Let me know if you need anything else."

Henry gazed into his glass of water, haunted by what the waitress had just said about her uncle's alleged encounter with an ape on Yonah Ridge. Eddy checked messages on his phone. Skip watched Tracy as she walked away.

***

Friday morning dawned clear and the low humidity of fall lent a briskness to the air although the weather forecast promised another quick warm up to eighty degrees. But the yellowing leaves on the hickories and beech were harbingers of the change in seasons as the green riot of Summer's photosynthesis succumbed to the fiery pageant of Autumn leaves and then the long grey sleep under Winter's blanketed sky. Meditating over a travel mug of black coffee, Henry's mind lingered on a phrase he had seen once in a book of quotations. "Autumn arrives in the early morning...". The rest of the quote said something about spring but the fading goldenrod nodded an emphatic testament to the fact that Spring was a long time away.

The trio of surveyors were a little giddy with it being Friday and knowing they would get paid for some windshield time on the ride back to Nashville. They drove out the now familiar dirt road up the hollow. Eddy jumped out and opened the gate and they drove across a pasture where white Charolais cattle looked on with cud-chewing blank stares. They stopped by the trail they had chopped out earlier in the week. Time to jump into the woods and get to work. Skip stretched out his full six-foot-four-inch frame, arching his back to wear off the stiffness of morning and age. Henry and Eddy gathered machetes, pink ribbon, stakes, and assorted surveying gear into orange duffle bags.

"Well, let's get in and get 'er done," said Skip, throwing the yellow tripod legs over his shoulder. "I'm ready to get back to town. I'm gettin' too old for all these travel gigs. These days are just too long."

"Amen," said Henry. "I'm ready to sit at my house for a change."

"Must be nice," said Eddy. "This time tomorrow I'll be headed up to Indiana."

"I suppose that's the price of being a rock star," said Skip. "Are you gonna be gone all next week?"

"Our last show is Tuesday night in Louisville. I'll be in next Thursday and Friday."

"Right on," said Skip.

Skip and Eddy had seemed to have forgotten about Henry's encounter the previous evening, but with each step deeper into the woods, Henry's mind raced to the strange creature he had been face to face with just thirteen hours before. The story Tracy had told them last night about her uncle replayed again and again like an earworm accompanied by frightening images, courtesy of Henry's active imagination.

After twenty minutes of walking they reached the set up where Henry had found the deer carcass. What isn't there is harder to see than what is and, walking up to the point, Henry didn't think about the deer at first. Then he remembered it and wondered where the carcass had gone. He turned back to the others and asked, "Do ya'll notice anything different about this spot?"

"Uh, oh yeah...this is where that deer was yesterday," said Eddy.

"Something must have drug it off into the woods to eat it last night," said Skip. "But that don't make no sense. Buzzards and coyotes couldn't do that."

"Yeah. That's what I was thinking," said Henry. He jabbed his surveying rod into the ground and walked around the area, looking at the periphery. "And look around. There aren't any signs of something that big being drug across the ground."

"You're right, there ain't," said Skip. "Could have been your monster got it."

"Do you believe me now?" asked Henry.

"Well, that deer was here and now it's gone. Could have been somebody come up here and picked it up but I couldn't imagine anybody being hungry enough to eat an animal that obviously died from disease. So yeah, it beats the hell out of me," said Skip.

"Hmmm. Alright, well, let's get on around this boundary and get out of here. I'm ready to get back to Nashville." With that Henry shouldered his rod and walked on toward his last point.

As Skip set up the instrument Henry pulled out his machete and began chopping a new trail through the underbrush. As the sun climbed the sky its light vanquished shadows and warmed the forest. Henry began to sweat. As he chopped through a tangle of laurel he sensed that something in the woods was watching him. He pushed the thought from his mind and immersed himself in a happier thought: in a few hours he would be out of the woods and going home for the weekend.

Chapter 3

Nashville was bustling on Friday afternoon as Henry, Skip, and Eddy rolled into town just after three o'clock. Driving down 21st Avenue to their company's office they saw people sitting on the patios of restaurants and bars, taking advantage of the warm October sunshine. Cardboard skeletons and ghosts decorated many of the storefronts along the busy street.

Once they arrived at the office, all three began unloading gear and plugging in batteries in the back room. Richard Cummings, the owner of the firm, walked in and greeted them.

"We'll, how did the last leg of the boundary go today?" he asked.

"It went pretty smooth," replied Henry. "Skip worked his magic once again. We closed out within eight tenths. That's on the twenty thousand feet we've traversed over the past few weeks."

"Hell yeah, that's great," said Cummings. "You didn't run into the developer while you were out there did you?"

"No. Were they supposed to pay us a visit?" asked Henry.

"I wasn't sure. That Buddy MacFarland is a strange bird," said Cummings, his arms crossed and a grimace on his face. "He's real hot to get this boundary done so his offer on the property can go through. I think he's afraid Springwater might have something else in mind."

"Like what?"

"Well, deep in the center of that property is a big waterfall. It comes out of a cave and drops into a large sinkhole. You probably wouldn't run across it unless we were doing a topographic survey. I think the State has expressed an interest in buying the land if Springwater could cut them a good deal on it. You know, trade some profit for PR," said Cummings with a laugh.

"Yeah, I wish we would have known about the waterfall. I'd like to have seen that," said Henry.

"By God, Henry didn't tell you what he *did* see!" said Skip loudly.

"What was that?" asked Cummings, smiling.

"Nothing," said Henry, shaking his head.

"Nothing hell. Henry here said he saw a bigfoot last night at our last set up!" said Skip, putting his arm around Henry's shoulders.

"What?" asked Cummings, incredulous.

"It was something," said Henry, reluctantly. "It was in the shadows, but I saw its eyes. It looked like it was just over six feet tall and covered with hair." He took a deep breath. "I can't explain it."

"Wow," exclaimed Cummings. Turning to Eddy who was standing in the back of the room, "And you and Skip didn't see anything?"

"No sir. Nothing but a lot of woods for the last four days," said Eddy.

"That's right," said Cummings. "I bet ya'll are ready to get out of here. Come on in my office and let's take a celebratory shot if you'd like one and ya'll get on home."

"Well, I'd like that very much," said Skip. The three men followed Cummings into his office where he pulled out a bottle of Tennessee whiskey and set it on his desk. He offered each man a small paper cup and poured them a generous shot of the amber libation.

"Here's to a good week of work," said Cummings, lifting his cup.

"Here! Here!" said Henry, Skip, and Eddy as they each downed their shot.

"Alright, now ya'll go out and have a great weekend," said Cummings. As they turned to walk out he called to Henry. "Henry, can I talk with you for a minute?"

"Sure. What is it?"

"About this bigfoot thing. That's really intriguing. But I'd appreciate it if you didn't say anything to anybody about it."

"You don't want people to think your party chief is crazy?" asked Henry, smiling.

"No, I have every confidence in you," said Cummings sincerely. "It's just, like I said, this MacFarland cat is a strange bird. If anything we did raised the profile of that property, you know got it before the eye of the public, he'd probably have a fit. And I'm sure you know if we get the topo and construction surveying and everything else, this contract is going to lead to some really nice Christmas bonuses for a couple of years to come."

"Sure thing boss. I'd just as soon drop it myself. It was late. I was tired. It could have been anything." Henry and Cummings shook hands then Henry walked out the backdoor to his worn-out pickup truck. The job completed, the boss debriefed. The whiskey had unlocked the floodgates of relaxation and he allowed mental and physical exhaustion to overtake him.

Chapter 4

When Henry got home that evening he immediately lay down on his couch and fell asleep. Having not slept well the night before, he slept deeply now. For two hours he was oblivious to the reality around him and lived in dreams where the inner dragons of his cerebellum exercised his mind in fight or flight scenarios involving encounters with large apes in vast wastelands of woods and grassy savannahs. It was dark when he awoke with a start. He looked at the clock and saw that it was a quarter past seven. It being a Friday night he showered and dressed to go out. He drove a few blocks to a little pub that specialized in craft beer and Vanderbilt co-eds, especially ones who glowed with a little hippie-chic mystique.

The conversation swirled around him. Henry chit-chatted with some people he knew but he wasn't feeling it tonight. Bars are places where people sit around talking about nothing. Many of them chain smoking cigarettes as a way of fighting off the boredom that comes with sitting for hours doing nothing, talking without saying anything, ready to repeat the same conversations night after night.

And Henry was okay with that. There is a phase in the life of many a single man and woman when the bar is their community. It is a place to relax. When one finds the right watering hole it is a place to meet likeminded people who need to blow off the world for a few hours and engage in the collective inactivity of spending money to drink and be in the presence of other people trying to fill the same holes of loneliness and boredom. Most people you meet and talk to in bars will be forgotten as soon as either they or you move on, whether you've known them for years or just met them that night. But there are others with whom you forge real bonds, whose mutual interests create lasting friendships. But none of those people were there for Henry on this particular Friday night, so at ten o'clock he headed back home.

He awoke early the next morning, refreshed after having slept in his own bed for the first time in five days. Henry brewed a pot of coffee and had a breakfast of bacon with toast and honey. Afterwards he sat down at his computer to catch up on emails and pass time peeping into other people's lives on social media. But whatever he had seen on Yonah Ridge still stirred restlessly in his psyche. He could not forget the face, especially the eyes he had seen looking back at him from the shadows.

He did a quick search for "bigfoot tennessee" and a long list of websites popped up. He followed a link for a site called CryptoWatch. On an introductory page the site discussed the plausibility of a large hominid existing which had so far eluded scientific confirmation. Why had a carcass never been found? Why were there no credible photographs? Would it be ethical to shoot such a creature? etc... The site offered a list of bigfoot sightings by state. Henry read through sightings from Tennessee and was intrigued to find some as recent as this past spring. That sighting had been in White County, which bordered Lytle County where his own encounter had taken place. The report of the sighting described the stench and the reddish fur of the creature. This was all consistent to what Henry had seen, and smelled. At the bottom of the page Joseph Wheeler was identified as the investigator who had spoken with the person who had filed the report. In Wheeler's commentary, which accompanied the report of the sighting, he acknowledged the encounter seemed to be authentic, with the witness remaining consistent throughout every detail of the sighting. Furthermore, Wheeler's credentials were given as a "government official for the state of Tennessee".

Henry's mind raced at the possibility that other people had had encounters similar to his and just one county over. He wanted to let others know about his encounter but, remembering Cummings' request that he not discuss the situation, he didn't want to post it on a website. To keep from broadcasting what he had seen across the internet, Henry decided to email Joseph Wheeler directly.

Mr. Wheeler,

Through the CryptoWatch website I see that you investigate bigfoot sightings throughout Tennessee. I would like to discuss a strange encounter that happened to me this past week. For the sake of privacy and the interest of the client I was working for I would prefer to meet and discuss this over a cup of coffee if you are in the Nashville area. Otherwise I will tell you via email but must insist that the details remain between you and me. You can reply to this email or call me at the number below.

Sincerely,

Henry. (615) 555-5555

Chapter 5

Joseph Wheeler was taking advantage of the warm, Indian summer Saturday to till under the spent tomato vines, pepper plants, and denuded okra stalks in his backyard garden. Three years a widower, he was considered by those around him to be a contrary but genuinely good-hearted old man on the verge of retirement from his position as the director of Water Resources Division of the Tennessee Department of Environment and Conservation. Had his wife still been living he would have already been retired. But cancer doesn't ask us what our plans are before it steps in and turns our lives upside down. He had loved his wife dearly, still loved her and missed her every day. Joseph Wheeler did not look forward to the long, grey, and damp winter that would be setting in over the next few weeks. He relished the bright sun of this late October day and the opportunity to tie up the loose ends of his garden until the greening of Spring which seemed so far away.

Taking a break from his tilling, he fixed himself a glass of iced tea and sat on his front porch enjoying the autumn display of the orange and red sugar maples which lined the street of his quiet neighborhood. The flashing light on his cell phone caught his attention. He picked it up and, reading through bifocals, saw that he had an email from a Henry Davidson. "Don't know 'im," Wheeler said to himself as he opened the email and read it anyway. As vague as it was, Henry's email still intrigued him. Everything about his work with CryptoWatch captivated Wheeler. With his wife having passed and his children and grandchildren scattered around the country, the last couple of years had been hard for him, no companion to ride with him off into the sunset. But his interactions with people who believe they had seen something genuinely unexplainable encouraged Wheeler with the vitality of new experience. "Well, sounds like this fella thinks he saw something." Wheeler dialed Henry's number."

"Hello?"

"Yes, I'm calling for a Mr. Henry Davidson."

"That would be me."

"Mr. Davidson, this is Joseph Wheeler. I understand you had something you wanted to discuss with me."

"Mr. Wheeler! I didn't expect to hear from you so soon. Yes. What I emailed you about. Would you be able to meet me sometime this weekend?"

"Sure. I'm just cleaning up my garden right now but I'll be free this afternoon," said Wheeler.

"That's great. Do you live anywhere near the 12th South neighborhood?" asked Henry.

"I live in Oak Hills, it's not too far."

"Great! How about we meet at Java Gaia at three?"

"Java Gaia? Send me the address and I'll GPS it."

"Cool. I'll text you that address as soon as we hang up. I'm so excited to tell you my story. I really haven't been able to tell anyone else," said Henry, surprised at his own enthusiasm.

"Yes, that's what they all say. I guess it's the nature of the beast," replied Wheeler with the equanimity of a professional, all be it one whose area of expertise far eclipsed the realm of the ordinary.

***

Java Gaia is a laid back little coffee shop with a hippie vibe. Original artwork hangs on the wall, paintings of dubious quality but imbued with the artist's undeniable passion to create. Large women painted in fat brush strokes, blurred cityscapes, and paintings of trees, more impressionistic than botanically accurate. It's a good place to read on quiet rainy afternoons with a fresh cup of something hot, brewed with love and served with a smile. At ten 'til three Henry ordered a double shot Americano from a pretty barista with alluring green eyes, an impish smile, and auburn hair bobbed around her ears. He sat at a table by a window. He thumbed through a book of poetry that lay on the table but before he found a verse that caught his eye he saw a man walk in and look around as if he was looking for someone in particular. A man in his sixties, with a healthy paunch and wearing suspenders, all capped off by a thick shock of white hair, Henry guessed this would be the man he was wanting to talk to.

"Mr. Wheeler?" Henry asked, standing up and stepping toward the man.

"Yes. You must be Henry," said Wheeler, extending his hand.

"Here let me get you something to drink," said Henry stepping up to the counter. "What would you like?"

"Black coffee is fine with me," said Wheeler.

"Black coffee it is." Henry ordered a coffee from the green-eyed barista and gave her his best smile as he put his change in the tip jar.

Sitting down at the table Wheeler and Henry engaged in small talk for a minute or so about the nice weather but, judging by the way Henry fingered the handle of his coffee mug, Wheeler decided to get right to the point.

"So, Mr. Davidson, let's talk about what you emailed me about."

"Yeah, I guess that's why I asked you here. And please call me Henry."

"That's fine. And of course, you can call me Joe."

"Well, Mr. Wheeler, I mean Joe, I was surveying a large piece of land up on Yonah Ridge over in Lytle County this past week. Are you familiar with the Cumberland Plateau?"

"Yes, my wife and I used to love to go camping at several of the parks over that way. I believe at Yonah Ridge there is a remarkable waterfall but I haven't had the opportunity to see it."

"Oh cool. And that's right. My boss just told me about the waterfall yesterday. But we were only surveying the boundary so I didn't have a chance to explore the interior of the property."

"Yes. I'd like to visit it sometime," said Wheeler, enjoying his coffee but impatient to move the conversation along.

"Well anyway, three of us were up on Yonah Ridge surveying a boundary all last week and everything was fairly routine. By Thursday afternoon we were all pretty tired. We'd really been pushing hard to get done. Around dusk I ran across the carcass of a deer that looked like it had just died that day. There was no smell of decay or anything. I'd encountered two or three others like it over the course of the summer and contacted TWRA [Tennessee Wildlife Resources Agency] about it. They told me it was likely that the deer had died of the EHD virus. My point being it was just another dead deer."

"Were there any signs of trauma on the deer?" asked Wheeler.

"No sir. No trauma," said Henry energetically, talking fast now, caught up in his own narrative. "Well, where I found the deer was in an opening. I needed somewhere to set a new point for our survey and that looked like a good spot. After we set the point I turned and began scouting for the next leg of our traverse. After consulting an old deed, I saw that the property line turned down into the gorge. As I walked into the gorge I smelled an awful stench. I guessed that maybe it was another dead deer. But I couldn't get over the feeling that something was watching me. You know, just a gut feeling that I wasn't alone."

"Yes," Wheeler nodded in agreement.

"It was about then that I looked deep into the brush on the slope of the gorge and saw something looking back at me. I mean it was like a person. You know...something with intelligence watching what I did."

"Did you see the body of this creature?"

"Yeah, it was standing in the shadows and at an odd angle because of the slope but it looked to be about six or seven feet tall and covered with hair."

"And what did you do then?" asked Wheeler.

"I screamed. The creature turned and walked away down into the gorge," said Henry, looking down into his coffee, obviously unsettled by retelling his encounter.

"Did anyone else see the creature?"

"No. I told the other guys but you know, it was getting dark, there were lots of shadows. They were convinced I had seen a bear or a deer or something."

"You say they *were* convinced. Do they think differently now?"

"No, not really. But the next morning, when we walked back in to finish the survey, the deer that had been there the night before was gone. No bones, no fur, no disturbance where something might have dragged it into the brush. It was just gone."

"Like it had been picked up and carried away?" asked Wheeler, inwardly assessing Henry's story as a credible sighting.

"Exactly."

Wheeler rubbed the sides of his coffee mug for a moment and stared down at the table formulating a thought. "Mr. Davidson, Henry, I find what you've described to be very intriguing. There are many things we experience in our lives that we don't understand and often enough it is just because we haven't had the background that would enable us to understand. Henry, what is your educational background?"

"I have a forestry degree," said Henry, not sure where Wheeler was going with the question.

"Okay, so we've established you are an educated young man with a background in science. Past experience has taught you that what you saw couldn't be real, that such creatures don't exist. So you're first instinct to write off this creature you saw as a bear or deer or some other more plausible creature. Hell, you've told yourself that you were in deep shadows and maybe didn't see anything at all."

"Yeah, but -"

"But you can't convince yourself of these other explanations. In your heart of hearts, you believe, you *know* what you saw was real. Am I right Henry?" Wheeler pressed Henry like a prosecutor questions a defendant.

"Yes. That's why I had to talk to you," said Henry, his voice low with emotional vulnerability.

"I understand. And Henry, I believe you saw what you think you saw. I've been investigating these phenomena for over a decade. I've talked with dozens of people, especially people on the plateau. There is something out there Science has not yet described. No carcass has been found, no good, authenticated photograph has ever been taken. But being intangible doesn't mean something isn't real. Can you touch a memory? No. But you relive them every day. Our experiences are real Henry."

"So, what do we do now?"

"I'd like to visit the site with you. You know, look for hair samples, get a feel for the terrain, the history of the place as regards land clearing and logging and such."

"Yeah, that would be nice. I can take you right to the spot."

"Maybe we could find that waterfall while we're there."

"I'd like to see that too," said Henry. "I'm free all day next Saturday. How does that sound to you?"

"Works for me," said Wheeler.

"Next Saturday it is. Oh, and I just wanted to make sure," asked Henry, broaching the subject as gingerly as possible, "you weren't planning to post a report of my testimony on your website, were you?"

"No. You came to me in confidence and I will honor that."

"Great. Thanks."

Chapter 6

Saturday morning, Halloween, dawned sunny and cool but a southerly breeze carried the promise of a warm afternoon. Henry met Wheeler at Java Gaia where they had first talked over coffee a week before. Henry pulled his decade old Ford pick-up into the parking lot and saw Wheeler standing beside his newish Buick SUV. "You're right on time," said Wheeler, looking at his watch. "I wondered if a single young man like yourself might have stayed out late on a Friday night." Henry smiled, shaking Wheeler's hand. "Well, I might be a little worse for wear but everybody at the bar was dressed up for Halloween last night and I wasn't so I called it an early night. Besides I'm anxious to hear what you think when we get over to Yonah Ridge today."

They walked inside the shop and were pleasantly greeted by a dreadlocked barista with a pierced septum and a bracelet tattooed on her wrist. Her hazel eyes and butterscotch skin spoke of the Creole beauty which might be the ultimate phenotype of human beings a thousand generations from now as all the peoples of the world easily move about, desegregate, procreate and the idea of race dissolves into a unified concept of what it looks like to be human. Despite this barista's exotic allure, Henry had hoped he'd see the green-eyed girl whose smile had caused him to flash his own boyish grin. Henry and Wheeler each ordered a black coffee and walked out to the parking lot and began discussing matters of navigation (as men will always do).

"The quickest way might be to go down and hit Four-forty to Twenty-four then pick up Eight-forty at Murfreesboro.

"That's what I had in mind," said Henry. "But I think instead of Eight-forty I'm going to take Ninety-six over to Highway Seventy at Liberty."

"Yes, that's a pretty drive," said Wheeler. "And then from

there I guess we'll go on through Smithville to Sparta?" asked Wheeler.

"That's right," replied Henry.

"How far is the property from Sparta? I'm vaguely familiar with the area but I can't pin point it exactly," said Wheeler.

"It's about ten or twelve miles out Seventy from Sparta, just over the county line."

"Okay, that's about what I thought. We'll be going through Bon Aqua," asked Wheeler, with a seemingly curious interest in whether or not they would pass by the handful of houses and one convenience store that represented all that was left of a little village that two hundred years ago had taken its moniker as a celebration of its sweet spring water.

"Yeah, the road we turn off on is just past Bon Aqua," replied Henry.

"Well, that explains something for me," said Wheeler, smugly, looking out the window, waiting for the inevitable question.

"What do you mean?" asked Henry with a curious smile in his voice.

"Henry, I've received another report of a sighting. In that area," said Wheeler, very satisfied to have someone with whom he could share this new report of an encounter.

"Really? Do tell," said Henry, intrigued.

"This report came in Wednesday night from a fella who was out inspecting power lines, you know, make sure the trees and such aren't growing up into them."

"Where did he have his encounter?"

Wheeler paused a moment, then turned, looked Henry in the eye, and said, "Bon Aqua."

"Holy shit," said Henry.

"That was my initial reaction too." Wheeler took a sip of coffee. "Henry, two sightings in a week within just a few miles of each other. I think we have us a legitimate cryptozoological event on our hands."

After an hour and a half of driving Henry turned off the highway onto a poorly paved road that followed a large creek. After three more miles he turned again onto a dirt road that followed a narrow creek up a hollow. The road ended at a cattle grate on the other side of which was a small driveway and a pasture. Henry drove across the pasture to a small opening in the woods at the mouth of a wet weather creek. "Well, this is it," he said, turning off the engine and opening his door. "It's a beautiful little valley back here," said Wheeler. "What did you say this is going to become? A shopping complex?"

"I'm not exactly sure but I heard it may be some kind of retail outlet. Of course, that's mostly hearsay. My boss says the developer is kind of an odd guy and has kept his intentions under his hat."

"I suppose he would. The Division of Natural Resources office is on the floor above mine. I've heard talk that they might be interested in purchasing this land. I'm not sure what your developer is offering as far as price, but giving the State a good deal on some scenic real estate with opportunities for hiking and camping would be great PR for the Springwater Paper Company."

"Yeah, that it would," replied Henry.

"How far along is it, the development?" asked Wheeler.

"Well, we just did the boundary which I think must have been required for purposes of securing a loan. As soon as we get the go ahead we'll start a topographic survey which will mean I spend a lot of time out here."

"Topographic? You have to measure all the elevations?"

"Elevations and any special features. I'll get the I-man to take a shot on me every fifty feet."

"Mercy! That could take forever. What did you say this was, a thousand acres?"

"Give or take. They might can get open areas with an aerial survey."

"So how long, conceivably, before someone could start building up here?" asked Wheeler.

"When the topo is done the engineers will take that survey and overlay their plans on it. I'd say we're a good two years away from groundbreaking," said Henry.

They set off into the woods, walking up the dry creek. "All this underbrush was thick as hell last week when we first got here. We had to chop every step until we got a ways up the hill," said Henry, waving his arm over the wilting bush honeysuckle on the ground.

"It looks like a lot of undergrowth. And plenty of sawbriers too," said Wheeler, wincing and pulling a quarter inch long thorn out of the back of his hand. "Hold up a second Henry," said Wheeler, kneeling down next to the barbed wire on a rusted fence. He pulled a vial from his back pack and, using the tweezers of his Swiss army knife, pulled a small tuft of hairs from one of the barbs and put them into the vial. "Probably just a deer," he said, zipping the backpack and slowly rising to his feet while steadying himself on Henry's arm.

"Will you do DNA analysis on those hairs?" asked Henry.

"We can if we need to. But we need something to compare it to if it looks out of the ordinary. I'm 99% positive this is deer hair," replied Wheeler.

The two men walked up the line that Henry and his crew had chopped out two weeks before. After thirty minutes they came to an opening. Henry stopped. "Here's where we found the deer carcass."

"The one that was there and then was gone the next morning?" asked Wheeler.

"Yes sir. It was after Skip took the shot on me here and I turned around to scout out our next set up is when I saw the creature. Down there just over the lip of the ridge."

Wheeler looked down in to the steep sided gorge. "That looks like some hellish terrain to try to work on," he said.

"It was pretty rough. Skip, he was the guy running the instrument, had to take a shot from a set-up midway down the slope while standing on his knees," said Henry, crouching uncomfortably down to the ground to demonstrate.

"Because the instrument had to be level I presume?" asked Wheeler.

"That's right. And he did a good job with it." Henry pointed down the hillside to indicate where the creature he saw had been standing on the slope. He and Wheeler investigated the spot for compressed earth, footprints, or any other signs of disturbance but found nothing. "This is the reason why people are reluctant to come forward to talk about an encounter," said Henry, frustrated. "You get back out here and of course there's nothing, not a sign of anything."

"That's how it goes I guess," said Wheeler, sympathetically. "Nature heals itself pretty quickly. Claw marks, footprints, and scratches on the earth don't persist long. And, as much chopping as you and your crew did out here, looking for broken twigs would be pointless."

"Well, what do you say we do? It's just after twelve noon," said Henry, reflexively looking at his watch.

"Let's walk back out to your truck and go find the trail head for that waterfall," said Wheeler, with the renewed vigor of having one mission completed, though unsuccessfully, and another about to be undertaken.

"Let's do that. Do you know where the trailhead is?" asked Henry.

"Not really, but I printed a map off the internet last night," said Wheeler, patting the front pocket of his shirt, indicating that is where he had stashed the map.

Back at Henry's truck they both took long swigs of water. Wheeler pulled a can of mixed nuts from his pack and offered some to Henry. "Thanks," said Henry.

"These are the fancy ones," said Wheeler, reading the can. "Less than 50% peanuts."

They drove back out to the main highway, paralleling the Calfkiller River for half a mile before turning onto another time worn blacktop that led them back in to the property. As the road gradually crumbled from asphalt to dirt it became narrower, eventually closing in to one lane.

"Okay, pull over here," said Wheeler, consulting the map then looking up. "It says park at the first wide spot after the road turns to dirt."

Henry parked with one wheel in a shallow ditch. They got of the truck and saw a small opening in the tangled branches of the underbrush. "That must be the trail," said Henry. How far is it?"

"This doesn't give a distance but it says it's about a thirty-minute walk."

"Well let's go see it," said Henry with enthusiasm. They walked quietly along the trail enjoying the dry acrid odor of autumn leaves and the humus smell of the forest floor. The woods were healthy here, not fouled by the cluttered understory caused by exotic invasive plants such as privet and bush honeysuckle. Near the dripping mouth of a large cave they came to a gigantic (by deciduous standards) tree. Nearby stones had been arranged into circles and inside each were the charred remains of recent campfires.

"That is a helluva big tree," said Wheeler, looking up. "Wonder what kind it is? Those leave are so high up I can't see 'em."

"I'm not sure," confessed Henry. "It's got fairly smooth bark. But it's not a beech. Looks like it's got simple leaves."

36

"Well I be damned! It's a buckeye," said Wheeler, bending to pick up a mahogany colored, one-inch round nut with a characteristic light spot on the bottom."

"Wow, biggest one I've ever seen," said Henry.

"Here," said Wheeler, handing the buckeye to Henry. "Put that in your pocket for good luck."

"Thanks," said Henry, feeling oddly touched by the simple offering.

They walked on a few more minutes with each man now beginning to feel the pangs of hunger from a morning spent in the woods. Contrary to what Wheeler's internet map had predicted they had already been walking for forty-five minutes and the switchbacked, undulating terrain was more challenging than either had expected. Then abruptly Henry motioned for them to stop for a moment. Cocking his head he said, "Hear that? It sounds like falling water."

Wheeler cocked his head, straining to hear. "I don't hear it, but I'm deaf in one ear and can't hear out of the other."

"It must be the waterfall." They walked with a renewed pep in their step, buoyed on by the promise of the waterfall close by.

Coming around a bend midway up the hillside they saw it, a falling sheet of water at the head of a narrow hollow. The waterfall was approximately 110 feet high. Autumn being the driest time of year in Tennessee, the flow was low. Looking down Henry and Wheeler could see that the water fell into a large sink area strewn with boulders the size of automobiles. The falls was encompassed by an impressive amphitheater rimmed by old growth hemlock and tulip poplar.

"This is absolutely beautiful," said Wheeler, continuing to look at the falls as he spoke to Henry. "Notice there is no creek down there for the water to fall in to."

"Yeah, I've never seen that before," said Henry. "Do you think it falls into a cave?"

"Not exactly. It a feature called a sink. Its earth with a lot of crevices in it. Looks like there's a mesh of muck and leaf litter over it. The water goes right through that and flows between the spaces in the boulders. Then underground. There's probably a big cavern under there."

"Geology is fascinating," exclaimed Henry. "Do you know if this falls has a name?"

"Virgin Falls," said Wheeler.

"Hmmm. It's interesting how things like waterfalls and other places get their names."

"I'd say it was some lonely surveyor that named it," said Wheeler. "Just like the Grand Tetons." Henry shot a confused glance at Wheeler. Noticing Henry's questioning eyes, Wheeler elaborated, "Surveyors named a lot of natural features around the country. They were often the first white person to see them. By the time they had got to something worth naming, they had likely been out for months on an expedition with a bunch of ugly men for company. Hence names like the Grand Tetons and such."

The two men walked on around the hill toward where it converged with the other side of the hollow and made a short ascent to the top of the waterfall. The falls emerged from a good-sized cave, its mouth twenty feet wide and perhaps twelve feet tall. The water flowed about thirty feet then fell over the precipice, crashing to the boulders below. It being the dry season and the water level low, Henry walked out to the edge of the falls and looked over. The rock was slick. Henry's boot slipped giving him a mild shudder as he stepped back from the ledge. "That's slick," he said.

"It's probably got *Spirogyra* or some other green algae growin' on it. That stuff's slicker than whale shit."

"It sure is. I've slipped more than once on it out wading creeks for smallmouth," said Henry.

Each man stood quietly atop the waterfall contemplating the scene. "I wonder what the developer has in mind for this spot?" asked Wheeler.

"I don't know. I'm not even sure whether or not he knows this waterfall is here." Henry looked down at the wildness of the forest below. "What do you think Mr. Wheeler? Should I tell somebody else? I mean here's this beautiful, unique waterfall, a virgin forest up in this hollow, and some very incredible creature out there that calls this place home."

"Who would you tell?" asked Wheeler.

"I feel like I should tell everybody. I want to share my experience."

"Who'd believe you," asked Wheeler, offering advice by asking questions.

"Nobody." After a moment of introspection Henry looked at his watch. "It's almost two. What do you say we hike out and go find us some lunch?"

"Sounds good to me. I'm starving."

"There's a place back in town we ate at a few times when we were working over here. They've got great burgers."

Chapter 7

At three o'clock Henry and Wheeler walked into the Ridgeline. They sat down at a table with a Formica top. The table was situated next to a window that looked out into the gravel parking lot. Dust stirred every time another truck (it was usually trucks) pulled in or out. The brown haired, faded jean clad waitress from two weeks before remembered Henry and greeted him as she walked over to the table. "Well, look whose back," she said. "Have you been out here working on Yonah Ridge again?"

"No, just out there looking around. This is my friend, Mr. Wheeler," said Henry, gesturing toward Wheeler, still not comfortable with calling him Joe. "He told me about a nice waterfall out there so we decided to drive over and check it out."

"Well how d'ya' do? I'm Tracy." Wheeler nodded with a shy smile. "What can I get you gentlemen to drink this afternoon?"

"I'll have water," said Henry.

"That's right and you take that with lemon, don't you?" asked Tracy.

"Yes, ma'am I do," replied Henry.

"And what will you have hun?" she asked, turning to Wheeler.

"I'll have a water and a cup of coffee," said Wheeler, fiddling with the silverware on the table.

"Alright, I'll be right back with your drinks and take your order," said Tracy with a hospitable smile as she turned and walked off.

"She's a very nice young lady," said Wheeler, watching as Tracy walked away, commenting on her pleasant demeanor and physical attributes simultaneously.

"Yeah, she was a sight for sore eyes at the end of some long, hot days out surveying," said Henry, with an unexplainable (he couldn't even explain it) twinge of melancholy.

"Well, so you recommend the burgers," commented Wheeler, turning to the menu.

"They're great!" said Henry, emphatically, confident that he was steering is friend in the right direction regarding a big decision. "Hand-pattied, good cheddar cheese...delicious."

Tracy walked back over with their drinks. "Alright, you boys decided what you want?"

They both ordered cheeseburgers and French fries, then chatted while they waited for their order.

"The one thing this place is missing is beer," said Henry. "A good cold one would hit the spot right now."

"Yeah, I sometimes miss having a cold beer. Very refreshing after a good day of work, or about anything else for that matter" said Wheeler, almost with a sense of nostalgia in his voice.

"Do you not drink anymore?"

"No, Henry, I haven't drank in seventeen years."

"Wow! That sounds specific. Did something happen to cause you to remember the day?" asked Henry.

"Alcoholics usually do."

"Oh, I'm sorry I said anything. I don't mean to pry," said Henry, trying to back away from the subject.

"No, no, it's okay," said Wheeler looking down at the table, taking a breath, collecting his thoughts for a moment before going into an explanation. "I was a bad whiskey drunk Henry. For years I just drank a few beers around the house, but then I got on the liquor and it got a-hold of me. I couldn't handle it. I'd get verbally abusive to my wife and started skipping work."

"I, I couldn't imagine you being that way," said Henry, sympathetically and with mild astonishment, although, in reality he hardly knew the man.

"That's because I'm not that way. There are demons in liquor, metaphorically, that inhabit our bodies in moments of weakness," said Wheeler, very serious.

"Did anything in particular happen that changed your drinking habits? And if it's none of my business please say so," said Henry.

"Yes, and yes, I feel very comfortable telling you." Wheeler nervously turned over the fork lying on the table as he collected his thoughts. "Henry, it was something I saw. Something only I saw and no one else who was with me. And no one would believe me, not even my wife, God rest her soul."

"What was it you saw?"

"We were camping on the plateau, down at Savage Gulf in 1991. It was a very remote area down in the gorge on a spur off the Fiery Gizzard Trail. Around dusk I was over at the creek scrubbing the last bits of supper out of mine and Lucy's camping dishes. Lucy was my wife's name. As I sat there splashing that water I heard something shuffle in the laurels that lined the creek. I imagined it was a raccoon or something that had been attracted to the smell of the food. I hoped it wasn't a bear," said Wheeler, looking up with a quick laugh. "Well, there was this smell and it wasn't good. I didn't know but what it wasn't the musk of some animal but I had no idea what kind. By this point my knees were hurting from kneeling, on top of a long day of hiking - that Fiery Gizzard is a rough trail - so I stood up and stretched. The blood kind of ran out of my head and I stumbled back just a little dizzy. Then I turned and saw it standing there on the creek bank about fifteen feet away. In the shadows, but just as real as those people at that table over there."

"What did it look like," asked Henry, captivated.

"You already know the answer to that Henry. You saw one yourself. Tall, covered with hair, orangutan-like face, intelligent eyes."

"So that's how you became interested in this Bigfoot, Sasquatch, whatever it is," said Henry with a sense of revelation.

"Yes, ultimately. But for a few years I just fought it, was angry that no one I trusted enough to tell would believe me. They believed I thought I had seen something but they didn't really think what I told them I saw was real. Eventually I held it inward. But when you have something you need to share you've either got to talk to people about it or pour poison on it till you kill it, or at least put it to sleep for a while. That's where the whiskey came in. Tennessee's finest psychiatrist or the devil's greatest ally. Not to everyone, but to me," Wheeler looked out the window into the gravel parking lot. "The way I treated my wife when I was drunk. I'll never forgive myself, but I know she did."

At this point Tracy brought the burgers to the table. Henry was relieved to break the tension and the melancholy that had cast a pall on Wheeler as he recalled his years as an alcoholic. "Well, I'm glad you're in a better place now," said Henry. "And I can't explain what a help you've been to me in dealing with this situation."

Wheeler bit into the cheeseburger and a small stream of juice ran out. "Oh mercy," he exclaimed, "that is some kind of good!"

After a few minutes Tracy came back to the table carrying a pitcher of water. "How is everything?" she asked.

"Fantastic," said Wheeler, wiping his mouth with a napkin.

"Well I'm glad you liked it." Turning to Henry, who had already finished his burger and was picking at the last of his French fries, "and it dudn't look like you have any complaints," she said, picking up his plate after Henry waved his hand over it signaling surrender. "Say, have you heard anything about what they've got planned out there on Yonah Ridge where ya'll of been working?"

"I've heard rumors of some sort of development but nothing too specific," said Henry, not sure how much he should divulge, although he too had only heard speculations.

"I've heard that they were gonna build a bunch of stores out there and maybe a theme park like Dollywood."

"Really?" said Henry, having never heard the theme park angle before.

"Sure 'nuff. A friend of mine was over at the high school waiting to see the principal about her kid and she heard him through the door on the phone talking about a big development. He's also the county executive, the principal."

"I'd heard the rumor of the outlet stores but nothing about the theme park," said Henry, knowing he would now become a quoted source of authority in the rumor mill of Lytle County. But he was beginning to feel there were larger issues at stake.

"And I've heard that the State is thinking about buying that land and turning it into a park," said Wheeler, to stir up the conversation.

"A park?" exclaimed Tracy, incredulous.

"Yes, that waterfall we visited today is quite lovely," said Wheeler.

"Yeah, I've heard it is real pretty," said Tracy. "I've not ever been back there to it. But I can't help but think we need some businesses to move in here more than we need a park. People are hurtin' for jobs around here," she said, emphatically.

"Where *is* there anywhere around here for people to work?" asked Henry. "I haven't really noticed any factories or much construction."

"There's a factory on the highway south of town that makes seats and visors for GM. But they laid off a bunch last spring. Most people around here drives to Cookeville for work. They's a few works over at the Nissan plant in Smyrna," said Tracy.

"That's a helluva long way to have to drive just to get to work," said Wheeler.

"It is. And I've known people that once they're car breaks down they lose their job," said Tracy, representing and relating the collective exasperation of an economically depressed community.

"It's a shame people can't find work close enough that they don't have to use half a paycheck in gas just going back and forth," said Henry.

"Yeah. And people in the city wonder why country people resort to making meth or growing pot," said Tracy. "I don't agree with it, I've seen what meth does to people. But you gotta make some money somehow."

"That's true. I suppose it's the same as my great-granddaddy up in Jackson County making moonshine during the Depression," said Henry.

"It's exactly the same," said Wheeler.

A moment's pause hung in the air as the conversation ran its short course, then Tracy picked up Wheeler's plate with a smile and said, "I'll be right back with your checks."

"And you can put his on mine," said Wheeler, gesturing toward Henry.

"I sure will hun," said Tracy as she turned and walk away with the plates.

Chapter 8

Henry and Wheeler each twisted tooth picks in their mouths, chewing on the pointy ends as they walked across the dusty parking lot back to Henry's truck. Driving through downtown they marveled at the early twentieth century buildings that stood on the square. What had been thriving retail space now housed antique stores, offices, or sat vacant.

"I've always thought these small-town squares could be revitalized with a couple of good restaurants," said Henry. "The Murfreesboro square is a lot of fun. It's got some interesting bars, good food. There's even some thriving retail stores."

"Murfreesboro is a helluva lot bigger with a helluva lot more money than all of Lytle County," said Wheeler. "Murfreesboro does have a pretty square but I suspect some of those business, especially the retail stores, are somebody's hobby, some rich man's way of keeping his wife entertained, letting her run a clothing boutique or health food store while he gets a good tax right off out of the deal."

"Could be. It's got to be hard being a mom-and-pop shop when you have two malls within three miles of your store," said Henry.

"I don't see how they do it," said Wheeler.

"What do you think about what Tracy said about needing a development that brings in jobs more than a park?" asked Henry. He had always had mixed feelings about this scenario and suspected Wheeler might have some good insight.

"I see her point," said Wheeler. "On the surface it almost seems arrogant to argue for a different point of view. These counties up here, especially Lytle County, are economically depressed areas. There's very little opportunity for employment.

People will stand in line up in Monterey waiting for a job picking guts out of a chicken carcass for a dollar above minimum wage and feel like they've found a good job."

"But parks do provide tax revenue from visitors passing through town," said Henry.

"Yes and no," said Wheeler. "The National Park Service had a real time with the locals expanding one of those parks up there, I think it was Denali. When they come in and take over an area they cut off everything: logging, grazing, mining, hunting - everything. There were threats of violence against rangers, the whole nine yards."

"Did this happen recently?" asked Henry.

"Oh yes, about 1980 or so, in your lifetime or close to it," said Wheeler.

"I missed it by about a year," said Henry smiling. "So what happened?"

"What always happens when the Federal government wants something. They get what they want. The Park Service expanded the park," declared Wheeler, flatly.

"It seems like it's turned out pretty well," said Henry. "I have some friends that spent a week in Denali a couple of years ago and loved it."

"They would, it's a beautiful place. My wife and I visited out there around 2003. And the economic impact of the park has been significant and remains so," said Wheeler.

"More so than logging or mining?"

"Hell yes. In the short run those extractive activities would have made a little money for a few people in the local area who were employed by the big corporations that control all that sort of thing, but then the jobs would have been phased out as the land was denuded. What then?" Wheeler rhetorically asked.

"Do you think the same scenario would apply to a state park on Yonah Ridge?" asked Henry.

"Not really," said Wheeler, matter-of-factly. "We're talking day hikers and over-night campers that would be drawn to such a park. Most would fill up their cars before leaving the town they live in and a bunch of 'em would bring trail mix and beef jerky from home."

"That's what I would do," said Henry. "So, you're guessing a creating a park here would have minimal economic impact for the community?"

"I don't see how it could even be close to what a bunch of retail outlets would bring in the form of jobs and tax revenue."

"What's the incentive for Lytle County to have a park established?"

"Hell, I can't see that there is any," said Wheeler. "It's a beautiful area and I feel a moral obligation as a citizen of the planet to preserve unspoiled nature for generations to come, but I can't expect someone who has to choose between a waterfall and a job to support his or her family to be too excited about my high-minded conservationist views."

"I remember having this conversation once with a logger out in California when I was visiting the Redwoods," said Henry. "He said, 'I resent people coming in here telling us how to use our land then going back to their comfortable house and tech-sector job in San Francisco or wherever while I'm sitting here out of work.' Obviously, I loved spending a couple of days camping and hiking around those amazing trees but I've always remembered what he said. He was a nice guy, you know, insightful, not some dude trying to play that blue-collar hero bullshit. And just like he said, I drove through, saw the redwoods, and went back to my home far away while there he sat without a job. It's complicated."

"It is," said Wheeler.

"So ultimately what is your view on creating a park around Virgin Falls?" asked Henry.

"I say preserve the land," said Wheeler frankly. "Building this outlet mall and paying somebody minimum wage to sell out-of-towners a bunch of foreign made crap they don't need is a band-aid on a larger economic problem."

"Some of those would be good jobs," said Henry, "management positions, facilities engineers. And what if it spawned more growth: restaurants, then more road building, more people moving in, residential building, the need for medical care? This could lead to a lot of jobs."

"It comes down to a land ethic Henry. I'm a conservationist. If people want a job bad enough or if they want a McDonalds and a Super Wal-Mart down the street from 'em, there's plenty of places they can move to that already have that. And, if they don't want to move, their kids probably will. Ultimately there are two camps in this debate and neither side has a perfect platform," confessed Wheeler.

They drove in silence for a minute while Henry digested what Wheeler had said. "From what I've heard about the scope of the project it sounds like it would destroy Yonah Ridge," said Henry. "Do you think if somehow undeniable proof of the existence of a large hominid could be presented people would be willing to set aside habitat for it? Or do you think they would be afraid and want to destroy it?"

Wheeler smiled at this question and thought for moment then answered, "Well, it would be curious to see how such a creature would be covered by the Endangered Species Act. I suspect that if proof of one of these creatures was put before the public eye, we'd have a frenzy on our hands. Primatologists, trophy hunters, and every curious person and nut job in between would be making their way to Lytle County to see a real, live Bigfoot. The media would have a circus with it," said Wheeler laughing.

"Yeah, it's almost too crazy to even think about," said Henry.

"But we've had two sightings here within a week," said Wheeler, with seriousness in his voice. "It may be something we're going to have to think about." Then, yawning he said, "But that's a discussion for another time. I think I'm going to rest my eyes for a minute. It's been a good long day." He leaned his head against the cab of the truck and fell asleep.

Chapter 9

The brightness of the day faded and with it the temperatures dipped in the clear night air of crystalline stars which foretold of a frosty morning to come. Perhaps that is why the crickets chirped so loudly as Jim Tyree and his new girlfriend, Treeva Saunders, sat on the front porch of his trailer enjoying a beer and a cigarette. An orange tabby cat sat on the rail around the deck licking its paw. They had just finished a dinner of rib-eye steaks and baked potatoes which Tyree had grilled on the fold-up charcoal grill that sat at a safe distance out in the yard, the coals having finally faded into a white clump of hot ashes.

"That steak was so good," said Treeva, rubbing Tyree's arm. "Thank you baby for cooking for us on Halloween."

"Ah, it was simple," replied Tyree. "I'm glad you enjoyed it. This is the way I like spending Halloween. It's a lot better than having to dress up in some silly outfit and standing around with a lot of other people doin' the same."

"I know, it's relaxing," she said. They sat quietly for another moment listening to the crickets in the darkness. Then Treeva reached into her jacket pocket and pulled out a small glass pipe. "Do you mind if I smoke a little?" she asked.

"No, that's fine," said Tyree, glancing toward her, then staring back out into the yard.

"You can have a hit if you'd like," she offered. "Its kind bud."

"No, I better not. They drug test us at work pretty regular. Sure as I hit that bowl my name would pop up for a pee test Monday morning."

"That just seems so unfair," said Treeva, "for them to monitor what you do on your own time. It's not like you're high out on the assembly line."

"I agree but that's just the way it is," said Tyree. "What's more unfair is for them to be paying me sixteen dollars an hour when I've been there for six years just because I'm contract labor when there's Nissan employees making eight and ten dollars an hour more than that working on the same line. That's what's hard for me to accept."

"I don't see how they get away with it," said Treeva.

"There's nobody to stop 'em. The middle class is dying and the politicians are working for the corporations. They're content to let the middle class go. They'll keep us on life support just long enough to make it look like the middle class died of old age. It's not just Nissan. It's across the board. But what can you do? A man's gotta work somewhere," said Tyree, taking a sip of beer and leaning back listening to the stereo playing through the open door. *"Sugar magnolia/ blossoms blooming..."*

Treeva took a big draw on the pipe, raising a puff of resinous, thick green smelling smoke. She exhaled and the cherry quickly faded in the bowl. *Ughm - Ughm* she coughed. "Well let's not think about that right now. Let's just enjoy our night," she said, laying the pipe on the table next to her then gently rubbing her hand up and down Tyree's arm.

"I agree," said Tyree, turning toward Treeva, leaning in, and softly kissing her. She giggled and he smiled as he picked her up and carried her inside.

"Oh Jim, where are you taking me?" she asked, imitating a damsel in distress.

"To the warm chambers of a pleasure palace m'lady," said Tyree, affecting an accent that was a cross between John Wayne and any random vendor at a Renaissance festival. The cat on the rail stopped licking its paw and eagerly eyed the abandoned dinner plates.

***

Tyree and Treeva lay in the intertwined comfort of post-coital bliss. A small fan hummed low across the room, stirring the air which was saturated with the smell of cigarettes and sex and that stale odor of burped beer as it is gaseously exhaled in deep sleep. With a start, as if from a dream, Tyree awoke and sat bolt upright in bed. Down the road he could hear his neighbor's coonhounds barking wildly in the night. "Must be a coon or possum," he thought.

He walked down the hall to the bathroom and relieved himself. He then walked to the kitchen and drew a glass of water from the faucet. As he drank the water, he felt the vibration of something rubbing against the side of his trailer. He grabbed his rifle out of the corner, reached to turn on the light but thought better of it, then walked out on the deck.

Peering into the darkness Tyree interrogated, "Who is out there? If anybody's there you better make yourself known." An uneasy silence was the only response to his call. Even the hounds had ceased their barking. The air was pregnant with the presence of another living being, one that was large, and knowing.

Treeva had heard Tyree's call into the darkness. "Jim, is everything okay?" she asked walking into the living room slipping Tyree's flannel shirt around her shoulders. Tyree turned and was momentarily distracted by her breasts, one of which was exposed and the partially concealed thigh which lured him with the erotic shadows cast by the bedroom lamp down the hall.

"Yeah, I guess," he said, stepping back inside. "Just thought I heard something."

"Surly you're not afraid of spooks on Halloween, are you?" asked Treeva, sticking her hands in his boxer shorts.

53

"No. But it is a night for mischief," said Tyree sitting down a minute to assess the situation. "You remember that ongoing saga I've had with Roberta's [Tyree's ex-wife] brother Royce?"

"You mean about the meth?"

"Yeah. He thinks I'm the one that got him busted for parole violation."

"Why does he think that?" asked Treeva, concerned, herself knowing Royce Rydell's violent nature.

"Because that's what Roberta told him. She did it as a form of psychological warfare against me, because she knows I know how damn crazy Royce is," said Tyree.

"Well baby, isn't he off in jail right now?" asked Treeva.

"I think so. But who's to say he didn't get some of his bunch to come down here and mess with me. I wouldn't put it past him to try to burn up my trailer."

"Should we call the sheriff?" asked Treeva.

"No, I really don't think it was anything. Those hounds finally quit barking. Let's just go back to sleep." Tyree rubbed his hand up Treeva's thigh and held her hand in his and gave her a reassuring kiss.

Tyree and Treeva climbed back into the cool sheets, tickling one another and giggling the lover's laugh. "I'm gonna by you a puppy," said Treeva. "You need a dog way out here to let you know when somebody comes around."

"Maybe I should just keep you here." Then suddenly, "Wait! Did you feel that? It felt like somebody hit the side of the trailer." Tyree looked at Treeva, placing his finger over his lips telling her to be quiet. He reached up and turned off the lamp.

"I feel it," whispered Treeva. "It feels like something leaning against the side of the trailer. What do you think it could be?"

"I don't know but I've had about enough of this." Tyree reached down and picked up the rifle which he had lain in the floor by the bed. Moving slowly in the darkness he walked to the bedroom window. Slowly he pulled back the edge of the closed blind -

"'AAAAHHHHHHH!" he screamed as he saw the creature just inches from his face, separated by a thin sheet of Plexiglas. It was a large human form with frayed flares of frizzed hair projecting from its head. In the darkness the face was indistinct but the haunting terror of unexplainable eyes looking back at Tyree filled the darkness, the looming gaze lent a strobe effect by the adrenaline infused imaginative talents of the human mind. Just as Tyree stood momentarily paralyzed by fear the creature was startled as well. It let out a piercing scream and banged the side of the trailer with its large hands. Tyree reflexively coiled back from the motion. Shaking badly, he picked up the rifle but the window was empty. The creature had already gone.

Treeva clung to Tyree, pulling on him, screaming, "Jim, what is it, what is it?" with tears and anguish over the unknown nature of this disaster in progress, the experience of second-hand panic and fear wearing at her psyche just as second-hand smoke violates the lungs of those not engaged in smoking.

"I... I don't know..." stammered Tyree, emotional, outraged, terrified. "I've never seen anything like it." He stood up and put on his blue jeans. "I'm gonna call the sheriff's department."

***

The human voice on the other end of the line had a calming effect on Tyree. He put on a pot of coffee then he and Treeva dressed and walked out on the deck and had a cigarette while waiting for someone to arrive. Thirty minutes later a green and white patrol car pulled up into the gravel driveway.

Chris Chumley was the newest deputy on Sheriff Wayne Case's four-man force. The fresh faced, red-headed deputy saw Tyree on the porch and opened the car door.

"You don't have no bitin' dogs out here do you Jim?" he asked before stepping out of the vehicle.

"No, not no more. I wouldn't have had to call you if I did," said Tyree, immediately dismissive of Chumley, remembering him from a few years before when Chumley had been a clumsy handed tight end on the high school football team.

"So what seems to have been the problem? 911 dispatch told me you had an intruder."

"Yeah, something like that," said Tyree brusquely, initiating the idiotic two step dance of male dominance which an older deputy would not have had to endure. "Somebody snooping around the yard then leaning up against the trailer looking in the windows. Lucky they didn't get shot," he said, opening the latch on a little gate allowing the deputy access to the deck.

"Did you see anyone or just hear them?" asked Chumley.

"I saw him, peekin' in my bedroom window," said Tyree, nodding his head toward the end of the trailer, giving a vague indication of direction.

"What did he look like?" asked Chumley.

"Big. Frizzy hair, bushy beard...looked a *hell* of a lot like Royce Rydell," said Tyree.

"You don't think he'd be coming around here messing with you do you Jim?" asked Chumley.

"Why the hell wouldn't I think that since my ex-wife, *his sister*, told him I was trying to get him put away again? It's Halloween. I know he's supposed to be in jail, but what if he had some of that bunch he runs with see how I'd respond to some trick or treat?" surmised Tyree.

"Maybe I'll have to pay Royce a visit and ask him about it," surmised Chumley. "He did just get out of jail. That parole violation got dismissed."

Tyree looked up with measured surprise to learn that Rydell was free. He sighed then said, "Don't go talk to him. No offense, but you need back up before you go up that holler after him. Anyway, that will just make matters worse." Tyree became less tense, took a sip of coffee, walked to the railing and looked out into the darkness. Treeva, who was still upset, lit another cigarette and sat without talking. "Besides, I'm not sure that it was him. I'm really not sure at all about what I saw."

"What do you mean?" asked Chumley, confused.

"I don't know. It must have been a big burly man but there was something different about him. Like something wild. He screamed when I saw him." There was a silence. Chumley decided to ask the other witness who had thus far been silent sitting in the shadows at the edge of the porch.

"Ma'am," started Chumley, then recognizing who the other person was, "Treeva is that you? I thought -"

"I didn't see anything," she said brusquely, cutting Chumley off in mid-sentence, irritated by the inevitable recognition, not wanting to have to explain it to Tyree. Several years before Treeva had provided the seventeen-year-old Chumley with his first sexual encounter. Back then she had worked at a little market and on Friday nights would sell beer to Chumley and his underage friends. "And no, I didn't see it," she said. "But I could feel it here, leaning against the trailer."

"Jim could this have clouded your vision about what you saw?" Tyree turned around to find Deputy Chumley holding the glass pipe. "You know this is paraphernalia and I'm supposed to give you a ticket."

A sudden, unforeseen feeling of disgust and frustration swept over Tyree and he took a step toward Chumley and in a low voice growled, "I'm talking about something a hell of a lot more important than a simple pot charge. There was something outside my trailer tonight that I don't know what the hell it was. It could have been a strung-out drug addict who wants to kill me or it could have been something a whole hell of a lot more unexplainable than that! I've been trying to convince myself for the last hour but this thing wasn't human and it wasn't an animal. I don't know what the hell it was."

Taken aback, Chumley set the piece down. "Well Jim, just try to keep this inside. Seeing it puts me in an awkward situation."

"I understand." Tyree took the pipe and slipped it into his pocket. "Look Chumley, that's what I saw. Treeva and I really need to get some rest. It's been a long night."

"I understand. At least now we have an official report. I'll take a drive up the holler just to see if I see anything."

"Okay, thanks. Thanks for coming out," said Tyree, signing his name to the first official police report of a strange creature lurking around Yonah Ridge.

Chapter 10

The creature ran on all fours through the woods, adrenaline streaming "Go, go, go!" through his arteries and veins. His heart pumped the blood, his blood carried the oxygen that fueled the powerful body as he ran, crashing with explosive force through the underbrush, paying no notice to the greenbrier and sharp twigs that snagged on his shaggy haired body. He ran down the steep slope of the gorge partially upright, using the trunks of hemlocks to break himself on his manic descent toward his den. After a few minutes he reached the creek. He jumped across sandstone boulders with the blue brightness of the moon silhouetting his large, powerful body against the white ripple of crashing water rapids where the stream descended down through varied strata of geologic time, drawn by unseen forces to the older worlds in the valleys below.

At length the creature arrived at his den, the opening hidden behind a tangle of birch roots and rhododendron. He slipped through seemingly impossible tight spaces into the damp sand just above the water line. He crawled farther back in the opening, the floor of his lair elevating up and up as he climbed deeper into the side of the mountain, the pebbled trickle of water that had carved the cavern gurgling softly on its steady drip drip drip eons old mission carrying sediments out, leaving emptiness in its place. Then at last he was on dry ground, where a bed of hemlock boughs and fresh leaves formed a comfortable mat over loamy soil. He was safe, deep in the secure womb of the mountain. He was an inherently subterranean dweller who had spent years in this lair and had never been discovered by the others.

He fell asleep on his evergreen bed, warm, in a comfortable place, but unsettled. He was restless in his dreams, jerking to the rhythms of images and sounds and smells that drifted before his twitching eyes. It was the others. He was much more aware of them now. Dim feelings had once led to instinctive actions: running at their scent, the imperative to never be found out, the sensual instincts strung together as vague recollections that could be interpreted as memory. He had always lived with the instinct to never be discovered, to never betray his lurking presence in the shadows. But now he found himself drawn to the others, some self-preserving mechanism within him had been bypassed. And he felt rage at the shrieks with which he was greeted. Shrieks that pierced his ears and caused an involuntary reflex to silence this disturbance in his otherwise quiet forest life, even if it meant a direct confrontation with the others.

This new impulse had come over him during the course of the summer and, each time he felt it, the image of a deer sprang before his mind's eye. Something was connected. His collective subconscious told him something was wrong with the deer but he ate it anyway. Drawn to it, as if pulled by some new organism's DNA controlling his body. He had no way of conceiving that it was the virus, something so small, a seemingly insignificant collection of molecules. But the virus had slipped into his central nervous system. It produced a neurochemical that was the perfect lock-and-key fit with receptors in his brain which triggered neurons to send orders on how to behave up and down the chain of nerves, launching powerful muscles into action, activated by the spark of an electron. The receptors in his ganglia sought out this molecule, and once satiated, did its bidding.

The creature fitfully dreamt of the past. Then awoke in a rage, bolting up from his pallet of evergreen boughs, lashing out in the darkness, scattering the branches of his bed, banging with powerful fists against his earthen walls, causing the pebbles and sand of his lair to run like an upturned hour glass.

Chapter 11

Thurmond Raines parked his four-wheel ATV at the upper end of a steep logging road. The eighty-year-old trail was so gashed with deep ruts that even all-terrain vehicles could go no farther and now sapling trees had been growing for years, further blocking the trail. But seven decades is a long time. In the span of an average human life the surrounding timber had come of age and was ready to harvest and there was talk that the trail would once again be cleared as soon as a logging contract was negotiated with the Springwater Paper Company. But not today. Today Raines and his five-year-old son, Wesley, would walk out the remainder of the old trail to the deer stand he had built on the southeast slope of Yonah Ridge. Overlooking the Calfkiller River far below, the deer stand sat in a pretty spot. Though Raines wanted the deer and knew they were all over the ridge, he was most happy to be introducing his son to nature. Too young to safely handle a firearm, Wesley had at least come of age enough to be introduced to the life of a sportsman. The bond between father and son is not as easily nurtured in the confines of the home. It is a bond that needs open spaces to grow.

In today's world, where men and women have chosen the steady paycheck, debt, and convenience of hiring themselves out for work rather than the struggle of a life of subsistence farming, sons have no way of understanding the father's role as a provider. Obviously, mothers do the same, but they have an innate nurturing instinct that is not as easily expressed in men. Therefore, the bond between father and son has to be cultivated through special experience, unlike the natural bond of motherly affection. Though Raines provided for his family by working forty hours a week at the automobile factory the next county over, that was not obvious to his son. By taking Wesley hunting he could show him what it meant to be a provider. He could let him feel the chill of the November air and the uncomfortable winter dampness, gradually toughening the boy for his place in the world, doing it in a loving way that made happy memories for both of them.

And this particular Sunday afternoon *was* an uncomfortable day. After the warm fall with the sweetgum and sugar maples blazing on the hillsides, late November had turned cool and wet. A mat of leaves on the forest floor made each step treacherous as Raines and Wesley walked along, bundled warm in camouflage coveralls, as lingering rain drops dripped from the bare trees.

"Daddy, will the deer come out if it starts raining again?" asked Wesley.

"I don't think the rain bothers them too much," said Raines, patiently.

"Oh. I bet their fur keeps them warm."

"They run and play in the snow," said Raines with a smile, turning back to look at his son. "Now let's be quiet. We're getting close to our deer stand."

"Okay. We'll get a deer," Wesley whispered. Raines smiled. He knew that if they shot one that Wesley would cry, just like he had done thirty years before, the first time he saw his father kill a deer. He remembered how deer were so much less common back then. Killing one was a true rite of passage that took skill but also a lot of luck just to see one. Now deer were everywhere. Especially in towns, eating people's gardens and grazing on their front lawns. Raines wondered about the population explosion of both deer and turkey in the last twenty years. More people coming in, you'd think there would be less wildlife. Oddly, habitat destruction seemed to increase their numbers.

As they approached the stand and Raines mused about deer populations, a rank odor hit them in the face. "What's that smell daddy?" asked Wesley. "A skunk?"

"No. I don't think it's a skunk. I don't know what it could be," replied Raines. "But maybe it will help mask our scent and a big ole buck will come walking by."

This excited Wesley and in his loudest whisper he said, "I hope so!" Raines helped Wesley climb up into the stand. Once they were both up there Raines helped his son put on a harness and then clipped him to a short tether to keep him from falling to the ground. They sat together looking out over the river which flowed by steel blue under the flat grayness of the winter clouds. As they sat quietly in the stand, their breathing modified, the rhythm of their breath, even their heart beats, became one with the surrounding forest. As the afternoon passed the light gradually faded, imperceptibly. No deer came by.

"Daddy, where are the deer? Why don't they come out?" asked Wesley.

"They don't always come out. Sometimes we just sit in the woods and wonder where they are."

"But they have to eat. If we were here ever day one would have to come by," reasoned Wesley.

"Well, that's part of the challenge. Us and the deer being in the same place at the same time. Skill is being able to tip that balance in our favor," said Raines.

"I wish we had skill," said Wesley, frustrated.

"I wish we had more of it," said Raines, smiling putting his arm around his son. "But we do have this pretty view of the river."

"Uh-uh. We should've gone fishing," said Wesley, feeling for the first time that pang of disappointment that everyone experiences when the adventure doesn't live up to our anticipation of it. "Daddy, I've gotta pee."

"Okay. I don't much think we're gonna see a deer this evening anyway. Maybe that smell ran them off." At that moment a piercing whistle rang through the woods. An instant later Raines and Wesley were alarmed by the crack of twigs breaking and something heavy and powerful running through the woods in the mountain laurel behind them.

"Daddy what was that," asked Wesley, half scared, half excited.

"I don't know son," said Raines. Concerned, he looked around from the deer stand but saw nothing. He felt like they were being watched. It was an unsettling feeling. "I'm gonna go down and make sure that wasn't one of those bears we've been hearing about. Then I'll come up and get you. Keep your tether on till I get back up."

"Okay Daddy. Then I can pee when I get down."

"That's right," said Raines as he stepped onto the ladder and climbed down out of the tree stand.

As he stepped onto the leaf litter of the forest floor Raines sensed something shift nearby in a thicket of laurel. He drew his gun around from the sling on his shoulder and cautiously walked toward the thicket.

"Daddy, what's down there?" called Wesley from up on the stand. With the perceptiveness of a child he knew something wasn't as it should be, something unforeseen had arisen and he sensed his father's unease with the situation. "I'm scared."

"Don't be scared Wes. There's nothing in these woods that can hurt you except rattlesnakes and lightening."

At this instant a snarling growl reverberated through the forest as the creature burst forth with explosive fury toward Raines. In the blink of an eye the creature ripped off Raines' face by the ear and threw his convulsing body ten feet through the air where it crashed against a pair of poplar trees. Above, on the platform, Wesley screamed in terror, seeing the large ape-like creature mangle his father and maul the life from his body. Mercifully, he passed out a few seconds into the attack.

***

The boy came to in the last gloom of twilight. Cautiously peeking over the platform, he could see the lifeless form of his father's body crumpled between the two poplars. There was no sign of the creature. Wesley shook with fear and cold and began to cry. With his shaking hands he tried to undo the carabineer which tethered him to the deer stand but was unable to undo the clasp. He sank farther into his coveralls and stared out into the dark forest. In twenty minutes all light was gone. Perhaps harkening back to his early hominid ancestors, the boy took comfort in the darkness and felt a little safety up on the platform.

***

The phone jolted Kendall Raines awake in his easy chair where he had drifted off watching football on TV. He checked the caller ID and saw it was coming from his brother's house. "Hey, what's up?" he said, putting the phone to his ear.

"Kendall, have you heard from Thurmond? Him and Wesley haven't come back from deer hunting yet," said Kayla Raines. A well-built woman of thirty-two, she twisted a strand of her auburn hair around her finger in nervous energy over her growing concern for the whereabouts of her son and husband.

"No. I haven't heard anything from them," he said, still groggy from the nap. He looked down at his watch. Eight o'clock. "It's eight o'clock. Been dark for a long time. I'd imagine he'd've at least called you by now."

"He hasn't. When I call his cell phone it tells me that he's unavailable which means he's either out of range or still has it turned off. But there's no way they're still in the woods," said Kayla.

"No. I wouldn't think they would be. Did he go hunting over to Yonah Ridge?"

"Yeah. Would you mind picking me up so we can drive out and see if his truck is still there? I just think something must be wrong and it's going to be cold again tonight." Kayla was becoming really upset.

"Yeah, I'll come over and get you. I'm sure they're alright, but it's not like Thurmond not to call after he gets out of the woods. 'Specially with Wesley with him."

Fifteen minutes later Kendall pulled up outside the vinyl siding, stick-built home that Thurmond and Kayla had bought at a foreclosure auction two years before. "Thanks for coming Kendall," said Kayla who had been waiting at the door and immediately ran to the truck.

"Well, I want to find my errant brother as much as you do. It's just not like him not to call," said Kendall.

They drove through a traffic light, past the Dollar General store, and headed out of town on a winding two-lane road. With night the sky had cleared and a few stars twinkled in the atmosphere in air that promised a heavy frost by early morning. On the way out to Yonah Ridge Kayla did not say much, just sat fumbling with her cell phone that was already out of its service area, occasionally muttering, "I just hope they're alright."

***

Five miles out of town they turned onto Sinking Creek Road, a mix of crumbling asphalt, gravel, and potholes that led up the hollow below Yonah Ridge. At the wide spot on the shoulder where the logging road began Kendall's headlight cast a reflection onto a parked vehicle. He came to a stop, pulling up slowly over crackling gravel. "That's Thurmond's truck. They're still out here," he said.

"My God, what are they doing out here so late? Something must be wrong," said Kayla, putting her hand over her mouth and sobbing quietly.

"Yeah, it's dark and cold. We need to find them and make sure they're alright." Kendall checked his phone. "Good. I've got service. I'm calling the sheriff."

Twenty minutes later Deputy Chris Chumley pulled up alongside Kendall's truck. After a brief explanation of what was going on the two men headed into the woods together with high beamed flashlights while Kayla stayed at the truck in case Thurmond and Wesley returned. The going was slow in the cold night. The mucous in each man's nose felt sharp and hard from the chill. A half-moon bled down a faint hue of blue light which diffused prettily through the bare branches of the hickory and poplar.

The climb was steep. Kendall, a smoker, had to stop occasionally to catch his breath. Chumley, young and fresh faced, had grown up in the era of public service announcements that warned of the myriad hazards of smoking. None the less, the steep climb took its toll on his chair-fitting, sedentary thighs as well.

Apart from the heaviness of their breathing, the pair walked mostly in silence up the rutted trail. After about fifteen minutes Kendall stopped. "Thurmond's deer stand is on up at the top of the ridge. But if they're out here they should be able to hear us from here." Without waiting for a response from Chumley, he raised his hands, cupping them around his mouth like a megaphone. "Thurmond! Thurmond! Are you out here?"

Each man stood quietly with their heads cocked and ears turned up the trail, monitoring for any response. All they heard was the night. Night in a forest in winter where the silence lies heavy as doom, where not even a cricket is around to chirp in the cold stillness.

"Do you think they're still out here?" asked Chumley.

"I wouldn't have us both freezing our asses off out here in the dark if I didn't," replied Kendall, sharply, then easing, "I just hope they're okay."

They walked on a few more minutes before Kendall called out again. "Thurmond! Thurmond! Are you out here?" Again, each man cocked his head, listening intently. Again, only silence. "We can't be too far from the deer stand," said Kendall with a hint of resignation in his voice. "When we get there we can turn around and start again in the morning."

Then suddenly -

"Uncle Ken....Uncle Ken, I'm here...I'm here...please, I'm cold!" It was Wesley.

A shot of invigorating hope ran through Kendall and the scared call of the young boy shivering in the night put a new pep in Chumley's step as well.

"Okay Wesley, just keep talking to me and we'll find you."

"I will."

"Where's your daddy?" asked Chumley.

"Please, Uncle Ken. Uncle Ken." At this point they could tell the little boy was frantic with fear.

"I'm right here son," said Kendall. The flashlights picked up the reflection of the four-wheeler. "Wesley are you still in the stand?"

"I'm so scared. I'm cold"

"It's okay. I'm here." Kendall began climbing the ladder to the deer stand while Chumley stayed on the ground looking around the area with his flashlight. After a moment the light flashed across the twin poplars and the beam came to rest on the dark shadow of

Thurmond Raines. Congealed blood covered what had been his face and the leaf litter on the ground. Chumley ran over to the body and sank to his knees, vomiting.

"Oh god, oh god. What has done this?" he screamed into the night. This was the first time the young deputy had ever experienced the truly grotesque, the manglement of good order and what is right, lost to the chaos of what can't be known or understood by those who are not lacking in humanity or do not know the true brutality of one living thing struggling against another when both are fighting for their lives.

"What is it?" asked Kendall, holding Wesley, who had collapsed into his arms.

"It's Thurmond. He's dead. Something terrible has happened," cried Chumley.

Young Wesley sobbed, vacantly as if in a trance, and Kendall knew that he would not ask him what he had seen for a long time. Frigid with the cold, the boy was obviously traumatized. This mystery would take time to unravel. For the time being the most important matter was reuniting a worried mother with her scared little boy.

***

As morning dawned a small group of pick-ups and two patrol cars were already parked on the gravel shoulder at the mouth of the logging road. Sheriff Wayne Case poured a last shot of steaming coffee out of a thermos into the threaded cup that screwed to the top. He sipped it slowly. A tall man with graying blonde hair, Case would have stood out as the authority figure in the group of men assembled even without his uniform and distinctive badge patch on his coat. Deputy Chumley, whose badge patch was slightly less elaborate, clicked a flashlight on and off a few times in nervous fidgeting. Kendall Raines stood off to the side talking on his cell phone. "Okay. At least he's getting some rest. We're about to head into the woods and bring Thurmond out. You get some rest too while he's sleeping." He ended the call and slipped his phone back into his pocket. Turning to the sheriff he sighed with fatigue and resignation.

"How's little Wesley doing?" asked Case.

"They gave him a sedative at the hospital. He's sleeping right now," replied Kendall.

"Does Kayla think he's likely to talk today?" asked Case.

"I doubt it," said Kendall. "And please Wayne, let's not push it. Something very bad happened out here yesterday. I just want to go get my brother out of the woods right now."

"I understand," said Case. At this point the muffled pre-dawn conversations were interrupted by the crackling of tires on gravel as Luke Sudderth and Jim Gaither pulled up in the Lytle County Emergency Medical Services ambulance. Case exchanged greetings with them as they exited their vehicle, then, turning to the other men who stood off at a little distance shuffling the keys and change in their pockets, he said, "Alright men. Thanks for coming out to help us this morning. Marty, help Luke and Jim grab that stretcher. Let's go recover this man."

"Why dudn't Chumley have to carry the stretcher?" asked Marty.

"He'll get his turn on the way out," said Case, with authority.

The men walked slowly up the steep and treacherous rutted road. They walked in silence in the morning's gloaming, apprehensive about what they would find. A new experience for each, this recovery of a mangled body. Luke Sudderth had served in Afghanistan and had some preconceptions of what he might find. But he knew he couldn't be sure. Bullets and shrapnel made their own kinds of wounds to human flesh. From what Chumley had described to them, this would be more organic. Damage inflicted by flesh on flesh. Primal. The succumbing of one life to the muscle and sinew of another.

The walk up the logging road seemed to go much more quickly to Kendall than it had the night before. First of all, there was daylight. Secondly, he already knew what he was looking for. He walked ahead of the other men. Determined to recover his brother's body and rescue him from the indignity of being dead in the woods at the mercy of the elements and subject to the inquiries of scavenging animals. After a few minutes Kendall saw his brother's four-wheeler up ahead. Turning back to the others who trudged more slowly he said, "Okay, we're here." He walked on up to the four-wheeler and turned the key. It started. He let the machine idle as he walked over to Thurmond's body. His initial reaction came from the gut, cringing at the mix of muscle and congealed blood that had been his brother's face. "Goddamn!" he muttered as a red flash of rage swept over him, but immediately dissipated into sentimentality. He pulled the blue handkerchief from his pocket and put it over Thurmond's face. A fleeting tear came to his eye. He wiped it away. By now the others had walked over to where he was standing.

"Holy shit!" said Jim, mouth agape, reacting to the broken, twisted body of Thurmond Raines. He had not seen the absent face.

Kendall turned to him with heat and snapped, "Hold your commentary Jim."

"I'm sorry Kendall. I - I -just..."

"I understand. It's rough," said Kendall.

At this point Case stepped in. "Okay Kendall, let me take over. You know we're going to do everything with respect for your brother."

"I appreciate that," said Kendall. "Let's just get him down off this godforsaken ridge. I need to get back and take care of the living. Kayla and Wesley."

"That's right Kendall. That's what we're going to do," said Case, his hand on Kendall's shoulder. Turning to the other's he began directing the recovery operation. "Chumley, you and Luke…".

Chapter 12

Iris Devonkamp was the third best looking reporter on Nashville evening news broadcasts. Moreover, she came across as the most intelligent in a smart lot of young reporters and had far and away the best diction. And she was good. A website had been established ranking the "hotness" of television news and weather personalities. It was visited and maintained by single men who cast votes for their favorites. Yes, such websites exist.

Iris had won accolades reporting news at a small television station in Missouri and had considered going to Mizzou to work on her masters in journalism. But when the job posted for a weeknight reporter in Nashville, Iris jumped at the opportunity. That had been two years ago. Now she was a well-known fixture on the evening news, "that pretty girl on Channel 3 that has a way with words".

Iris arrived at work Monday around noon. She dropped off her backpack, said hello to staff she passed in the hallway, then sat down in her cubicle to check email. She often got email from her stories, half of them loving the story, half hating it, nearly all complimentary of her journalistic skill and reporting acumen. And, of course, there were the occasional emails from strange men offering to take her out for a drink.

While Iris sat sorting through the emails, looking for potential story ideas, the newsroom director walked up and stuck his head into her cubicle. "Good afternoon Iris," he said, hastily. "Can you be ready to go in ten minutes?"

"Good afternoon," she replied, "and yes I suppose. What's going on?"

"A hunter was killed in Lytle County, way over on the plateau. Not sure what happened but it seems a little suspicious."

"Oh? Is there going to be a press conference?"

"Bingo," said the director, pointing his finger at Iris, pulling an imaginary trigger.

"What time?" she asked.

"Around three. Still waiting to hear if it's going to be at the site or if it will be at the sheriff's office. I'll text you before you get there and let you know."

***

Iris and the cameraman drove down the interstate in intermittent drizzle. The wipers creaked as they swept away mist on the windshield. At Smithville they left the Interstate and turned onto Highway 56, winding through the bare grey hills and dark trees. Iris' phone buzzed with a text from the news director:

> *Press conference is at the site. It's at three. Call sheriff's office for directions at 931-555-5555. Let me know if you have any questions.*

Iris dutifully called the number and was given directions to the scene where the press conference would be held. At 2:15 p.m. the cameraman pulled the large van with the broadcasting dish on top to the shoulder of the road at the mouth of the logging road. A smattering of local townsfolk was assembled, talking in small groups, casually kicking at the gravel of the road with the edge of their boots, shuffling the keys and change in their pockets, waiting. Two reporters from newspapers representing the surrounding counties were there as well. No other Nashville news stations were present and Iris, being an exceptionally ambitious journalist, was thrilled at the possibility of a *scoop*.

At ten till three a tall man in a beige and brown uniform walked out of the woods accompanied by a man wearing a grey and green uniform who sported a thick salt-and-pepper mustache which lent a certain distinction to his face. A man with dark thinning hair and black glasses, wearing khakis and a dark blue winter coat, walked with them. They gathered around the patrol cars for a moment where there was a flurry of activity that centered around a piece of paper as if the men were comparing notes. Then at 3:01 the tall man in the brown and beige uniform walked up to where the townsfolk and reporters had gathered. A large spotlight from the TV cameraman caused him to squint his eyes at first but, recovering, he began to speak without a microphone:

"Good afternoon, such as it is. I'm Sheriff Wayne Case with the Lytle County Sheriff's Department. As you know a hunter, Thurmond Raines, was killed near his deer stand approximately half a mile up the logging road behind me, near the top of Yonah Ridge. Without going into too much detail, the nature of his injuries can only be described as horrific. There is no sign that Mr. Raines died of any sort of gunshot wound. It looks as though he may have been the victim of a wild animal attack. Officer David Hix [gestures to the man with the mustache] is a representative from the TWRA [Tennessee Wildlife Resources Agency]. I have been consulting with him this afternoon to try and figure out any animal that might have done this. At this time, we don't have any real idea. Officer Hix has collected fur samples from some fences around here to see if there's any chance that perhaps a bear or mountain lion might be in the area. He assures me that the chances of either of these animals being present in this area are slim but not out of the question. As we learn more, we will keep you posted." Sheriff Case and the others turned and began to walk out of the spotlights.

"Sheriff Case, question please -" injected Iris. Case turned slowly, immediately noticing Iris, who was leaning in toward him.

"Just one or two," he said, impatiently.

"Iris Devonkamp, Channel 3 News," she said, introducing herself, then asked, "Have you found any tracks or anything that would indicate that this was an animal attack and not a murder?"

"No. Not at this time," replied Case, curtly.

"Then how can you rule out the possibility of foul play?" asked Iris.

"Miss Devonkamp, there's nothing to indicate a human did or even could have done this," said Case, bluntly.

"But sheriff -"

"That's all for now. Thank you," said Case as he looked at the other men who had been with him and walked back to their cars.

"He's not telling us everything," said Iris, turning to the cameraman. She milled about the crowd a moment talking to the two newspaper reporters when suddenly a man walked up to her brusquely.

"You say you're with Channel 3 News?" It was Kendall Raines.

"Yes, that's right," said Iris, caught off guard.

"Thurmond Raines was my brother. Can I talk to you for a minute, in private?"

"Yes, of course," she replied, thrilled at the possibility of getting a different side of the story. As the two of them stepped away from the group, Kendall Raines self-consciously looked over his shoulder to see if anyone had noticed him talking with a reporter.

"Look, Miss -" he hesitated not remembering her name.

"Devonkamp, Iris Devonkamp," she replied helpfully.

"Look Miss Devonkamp, there's something really wrong about what happened out here to my brother. The sheriff is a good man and I know he's trying not to raise a panic if there's nothing to panic about. But there's something loose in those woods that broke my brother's body like toothpicks and ripped his face off his head." Raines gasped with emotion then went on, "There's gonna be hunters, maybe hikers, there's a waterfall back there. There's gonna be more people in these woods."

"I see," said Iris, concerned. "Would you like me to say more than what the sheriff said at the press conference?"

"I think people need to know the gravity of the situation," said Raines, his voice brittle with emotion.

"Mr. Raines, I assume people around here know you. Perhaps you could say something on camera. That might get more people's attention," said Iris, with empathy.

"Okay. I just don't want to look like a fool."

"You won't. And I can show you the final edit beforehand if you'd like."

Two hours later darkness had fallen on the scene as Iris prepared to post a live update on the story. The soggy forest added ambiance, dripping close at her back illuminated in the glow of a spotlight as the reporters at the anchor desk threw the story to her.

"*A deer hunter in Lytle County has been killed while his young son watched and still, no one knows exactly what happened. Iris Devonkamp is live on the scene with this report.*"

"Yeah, Demetria, it's a really sad story. This community is just in shock," said Iris. Then the producer cut to her taped report.

Thurmond Raines and his five-year-old son walked into these woods in Lytle County late yesterday to go deer hunting. What was supposed to be a happy father-and-son afternoon turned tragic and authorities are still trying to figure out what happened.

Kendall Raines, the victim's brother describes a hectic call from his sister-in-law.

KENDALL RAINES (INTERVIEW) - "Kayla called me and asked if I'd seen or heard from Thurmond. It was way after dark and him and Wesley should have been home or at least called her by then. I told her I'd pick her up and we'd go look for them...I pretty much knew where he was hunting. We got there, saw his truck still parked there on the side of the road and figured he may have had an accident or something. I called the sheriff's department and me and a deputy walked up and found the deer stand and my brother laying off to the side dead. He was mangled. [HIS VOICE BREAKS]. The only reason I'm talking about it is because we need to find who or what did this."

Sheriff Wayne Case held a press conference Monday afternoon.

SHERIFF CASE SOUNDBITE - "the nature of his injuries can only be described as horrific. There is no sign that Mr. Raines died of any sort of gunshot wound. It looks as though he may have been the victim of a wild animal attack. Officer David Hix is a representative from the TWRA. I have been consulting with him this afternoon to try and figure out any animal that might have done this. At this time, we don't have any real idea."

No one knows exactly what happened to Thurmond Raines but whatever it was has got this small community on edge. In Lytle County, Iris Deveonkamp reporting for Channel 3 News.

Cut back to live feed of Iris standing in front of the camera with the dripping woods behind her.

"Iris, has the little boy been able to provide any information about what he saw?" asked the anchor.

"No Demetria. When I spoke with Kendall Raines, the little boy's uncle, he said that he is too distraught and that his mother only wants him to rest."

"Such a sad story, I'm sure there will be more details to follow that provides some explanation," said the anchor, then, turning back to the camera, *"In happier news…"*

Chapter 13

Buddy MacFarland sipped a scotch with three ice cubes in it as he watched the news report describing the mysterious death of a deer hunter on Yonah Ridge. A sense of panic passed over him as he listened to the details, vague as they were. A possible animal attack. Ongoing investigation.

His company, MacFarland Enterprises, was deep in negotiations to purchase the property where the attack had taken place. One thousand acres of second and third growth hardwood forest currently owned by the Springwater Paper Company. He poured another two fingers of scotch into his glass. This could have bad implications. Raising the profile of land that had already attracted the attention of a conservation group called Friends of the Cumberlands. "It's that damn waterfall," thought MacFarland. The group had described it as a treasure of Tennessee's natural heritage. Through the lobbying efforts of Friends of the Cumberlands, the Tennessee Department of Environment and Conservation and the Nature Conservancy had already taken interest in purchasing the property to preserve it for conservation and low impact recreational use.

MacFarland's goal was to snatch up the land from Springwater before it could be locked away forever by conservationists. His plan was to take advantage of the dirt-cheap price of the land and develop the area, log the good timber then knock down the remaining trees, blast away the undulating terrain into level parking lots, build a hundred thousand square foot cinder block boxes and court outlet stores to come fill it up. He touted his idea as providing an economic shot in the arm to a depressed region. His *piece de resistance* for the portly set was to build the Kuntry Kitchen mother store, complete with the world's largest buffet of fried meats and pork-fat infused vegetables. His promise of jobs and tax revenue was an easy sell to the locals, who had few opportunities for a good job with benefits.

But get the big city tree-huggers involved and he'd have a fight on his hands. Yes, he had to go into damage control mode right now. He pulled out his cell phone and called the head man in Lytle County.

Jimmy Finney was the county executive, high school principal, and was the third man at the press conference, standing next to David Hix as Sheriff Case delivered their carefully crafted, unified statement. He had just got home and draped his dark blue coat on the back of his chair and was about to sit down to a dinner of salmon patties, stewed potatoes, and green beans with his wife and two children when the phone rang. "Ummm…they always call right as we sit down to dinner," he said, taking a sip of tea and walking over to answer the phone on the wall. "This is Jimmy," he said, putting the receiver to his ear.

"Jimmy, Buddy MacFarland here," said the developer, trying to sound nonchalant, like a man of affairs who is always cool and collected.

"Yes. What can I do for you Mr. MacFarland?"

"Oh Jimmy, please call me Buddy."

"Okay. What can I do for you Buddy?"

"Jimmy, I was just watching the news, saw you standing there beside your sheriff at that press conference. I see you had an incident yesterday with a hunter getting killed out on Yonah Ridge."

"Yes, it's been very upsetting. Thurmond Raines was a good man and leaves behind a wife and young son," said Finney.

"It is tragic," said MacFarland, then clearing his throat, "Look, I was just wondering who's handling the investigation?"

"Well, mostly Sheriff Case. Why do you ask?"

"Well, Jimmy, you know that is a sensitive piece of property up there. There are others interested in purchasing the land. People who may not have the economic interests of the community as their primary concern," insinuated MacFarland.

"I assume you mean the State and conservation groups wanting to turn the land into a park," said Finney.

"Exactly. As noble as their intentions might be, having all that land cut off from development won't help Lytle County a damn bit," blurted MacFarland.

"Buddy, I've had a long day out in the damp and cold, now my supper is getting cold. Can you please get to your point and maybe I can call you back?"

"Very well, I don't mean to keep you. But if you can guide any coverage of this story away from mentioning the waterfall back there on Yonah Ridge and downplay any potential interests from conservation groups I think we'll all be better off."

"Well Mr. MacFarland, I'll see what I can do. But we have to conduct a proper investigation."

"Of course," said MacFarland, a bit patronizingly.

"Mr. MacFarland, I don't think you understand the true implications of what has taken place. This isn't the first unexplainable incident we've had recently. Next time you come to visit I'll fill you in."

"What sort of incidents are you referring to?" demanded MacFarland, anxiously.

"Good night Mr. MacFarland. I'm going to eat my supper now." MacFarland kept the phone to his ear until he heard the "click" on the other end of the line. He dazedly looked at the television without paying attention to it. But if he had he would have seen an advertisement for beef jerky that featured an agitated Sasquatch. He reached for the bottle and poured two more fingers of scotch.

82

Chapter 14

Wesley Raines felt cold in the dampness and gray darkness of the evening twilight. He wished his father would return to the deer stand. He had never been out like this before. Alone in the dark, deep in the woods, far from the comfort of his mother and home. His father was down below, investigating a rustling sound in the dark woods near the base of the stand. Wesley looked and the sky was perceptibly darker than it had been just minutes before.

Then he saw his father standing before him, facing him as if he were about to speak. The shadows had clouded the familiar contours of his face and now light and dark played about the hollows of his eyes and beneath his nostrils giving him a clown-like, unsettling appearance.

"Daddy," called Wesley, seeking reassurance. As he did this a dark fluid, blood, began streaming down from his father's eyes. Any familiarity, any comfort the face may have held for young Wesley melted away, leaving the soulless eye sockets of a skeleton in their place.

That's when he became aware of the creature, large and hairy. With a swing of its large powerful arm it toppled the stiff, lifeless form of his father and then it focused its gleaming yellow eyes on Wesley with an intense gaze. It walked toward him, a rumbling growl coming from the creature as Wesley backed to the farthest corner of the deer stand –

"AAAAAAHHHHHHHHHH!!!!!!!" screamed the young boy waking abruptly to the florescent light and bright white tile of the hospital room. His mother, who had briefly dozed off, jumped, jarred awake by the boy's sudden scream.

"Wesley, Wesley," she cried. "I'm right here. It's Momma. I'm right here," she sobbed cradling young Wesley in her arms.

"Momma, the monster, the monster! It was coming to get me like it got Daddy," he sobbed.

"It's okay honey. It's okay," said Kayla, reassuringly. "It was only a dream."

"No it wasn't," sobbed Wesley. "The monster that got Daddy was coming to get me just now. It was coming to get me," he cried. Then he collapsed again into his mother's loving arms.

Chapter 15

Tuesday morning started off with a spike in Wheeler's blood pressure. He spit a mix of venom and coffee as he threw the field report down on his desk. "That son-of-a-bitch has been falsifying his turbidity readings for the last six months. With that kind of a carbon rich environment there's no telling what kind of bacteria is growing in that water. It's a wonder we haven't been getting calls from people who've gotten sick," he said, referring to the infractions of a water treatment plant operator on a small system in west Tennessee.

"What do you want to do? Fine him or go for a civil suit to take his license?" asked his young protégé, just out of college, another granola hippie kid who had studied biology because of his love for the outdoors, only to find himself saving the world from the fluorescent confines of a cubicle on the sixth floor of a high rise in downtown Nashville.

"I say we fine the hell out of him and maybe the county will fire his ass because he's a financial liability. This is his third infraction in six years."

Thus mentored, the fresh-faced assistant walked away from the cluttered corner office with the messy desk where Wheeler had presided as the Director of Water Resources for the past twelve years. Wheeler was still flustered when the phone rang with David Hix on the other end of the line.

"Water Resources, Wheeler speaking."

"Joe, this is David Hix, TWRA"

"Well how the hell are you? I don't think I've seen you since that GIS training back in the spring," said Wheeler, easily slipping back into his genial self again.

"I'm doing alright," replied Hix. "Getting ready to eat too much turkey," he added referring to the upcoming Thanksgiving holiday.

"I know how that goes," agreed Wheeler. "I'll be visiting my brother and his wife for turkey and football. What can I do for you?"

"Joe, have you heard anything about this situation out in Lytle County?"

"You mean the hunter that got killed? I saw something on the news about it last night. In fact, I think I saw you standing there at the press conference," said Wheeler with a good-natured smile in his voice.

"Yeah, that was me," said Hix, bashfully.

"Sounds like you and the sheriff up there are having a hard time figuring out what happened to that young man," said Wheeler, concerned.

"Yeah, all we can figure is that it's some kind of animal attack."

"So where do I come in?" asked Wheeler.

"Joe, I know you're part of that Bigfoot research outfit."

"Yes. What about it?" Wheeler asked, curious, not defensive.

"Well, I know I've never given it much credence in the past but I checked out your website this morning and read the entry you put in about that man with the power company who said he saw a bigfoot out in Bon Aqua," explained Hix.

"So, I assume you found something during your investigation that has piqued your curiosity," surmised Wheeler.

"Well, we've found some footprints that I'd like you to take a look at."

"Footprints?" asked Wheeler incredulous but excited.

"Yeah, I made a cast of one and we've taken precautions to make sure the area hasn't been disturbed. Do you think you could come out and take a look at it?"

"Today?" asked Wheeler, hopeful.

"Yes, today. I think time is of the essence," said Hix. "I've also collected some hairs from a nearby fence. They're not from a deer. These are longer and red."

"I should be able to come out there." said Wheeler. "I just have to give my deputy a list of things to do while I'm out."

"Good, I'll be looking forward to seeing you," said Hix. "And Joe, do you really believe that guy that said he saw some creature over in Bon Aqua?" Hix was seeking confirmation, as if to legitimize his own suspicions.

"I'll tell you David, I do believe him. He saw something. He wasn't some flighty nut job," confided Wheeler.

"Well. I was just wondering. You know the hunter had his kid with him," said Hix.

"Yes," said Wheeler. "As I recall he has been too upset to talk about it."

"Joe, keep this between you and me now, but the little boy *has* talked," confessed Hix in a hushed tone. "He kept saying something about a big, hairy monster coming out of the brush and attacking his dad. Please don't repeat that to anyone."

"So, do you believe that's what happened?" asked Wheeler.

"I don't know. I want to hear what you think. I want to see what happens when we get the DNA samples back," said Hix

"David, just one question on that," said Wheeler. "What the hell will you compare the samples to if you already know they aren't from a deer?"

"There's some follicle on these samples," said Hix. "I want to see if there is any trace of EHD virus."

"What would that have to do with anything? I've heard it's killed off some deer but otherwise-" started Wheeler but Hix cut him off.

"Joe, it's not just deer. A few weeks ago, some coyotes in Humphreys County were reported for killing some livestock, calves and goats, even a couple of goat dogs, you know, the big Pyrenees."

"Yes...," followed Wheeler.

"One of the farmers who witnessed it said the coyotes were acting exceptionally aggressive. He was able to shoot a couple of them. He knew their behavior was aberrant so he turned in the carcasses to a deer check in station where they put them on ice." Hix paused.

"Well go on David. Did your agency perform an autopsy?" asked Wheeler.

"We did. It turned out that all the brains contained a mutated form of the EHD virus."

"Oh mercy," said Wheeler. "So, you're afraid there may be some possibility, however slight, of a large hominid whose been infected by the virus?"

"It's a stretch, I know. But between the injury inflicted on Mr. Raines, what the kid has said, and the sighting you wrote about, I just don't know," sighed Hix.

"I'll be there this afternoon," said Wheeler, in scientific confederation with Hix, who had lost the luxury of preconceptions and denial in the face of mounting evidence for the existence of something he did not understand.

"And Joe," admonished Hix, "please don't tell anyone else."

"David, I'm afraid I have to tell one more person."

"But Joe, this is a sensitive matter. There's a lot at stake here," protested Hix. "A family has lost a husband and a father. They don't want to hear that the investigators are looking for Bigfoot as a possible suspect. And the developer, MacFarland. He wants to buy this land where the attack happened. He's a pain in the ass."

"David, I understand your situation. But there has been another encounter, just a couple of days before the one you read about. Only this one happened *on* Yonah Ridge," said Wheeler, with gravity in his voice.

"Holy shit!" responded Hix, a chill running down his spine.

"Yeah. A surveyor. Him and his crew were out there doing some work for your man MacFarland. I didn't post his report because, like you, he says MacFarland is a sensitive man. But now a man has been killed and the little boy has told you what killed him. We can only sit on this so long. But I'll see you this afternoon. I'll meet you at the Ridgeline," said Wheeler.

Wheeler hung up the phone and bit his finger as an emotional response at the realization that was slowly coming over him. The world was about to find out that a large hominid, unknown to science, did indeed exist. And he was going to be the conduit for sharing this knowledge with the world. He picked up his phone and dialed Henry's number.

Henry was working alone, using a GPS to collect data points which drafters in the office would use to draw a stretch of highway that was to be widened. Standing on the yellow line in the center of the road, Henry plumbed the rod on which the GPS was mounted then took a "shot" by hitting the enter key on the data collector. Just as the shot was taken Henry looked up to see a dump truck barreling down the road toward him. He quickly jumped to the shoulder. The truck never slowed down and Henry flipped the driver his middle finger as the truck blew by. As all this was happening Henry's phone rang. He answered, "Hello."

"Henry, its Joe."

"Oh hey Mr. Wheeler."

"I hate to bother you at work," said Wheeler.

"No that's fine," said Henry. "Just out here trying to dodge traffic."

"Well, be careful," said Wheeler. "What I was calling about was that attack that was on the news last night."

"Yeah. Have you heard anything else?" asked Henry.

"Henry, you're not going to believe this," said Wheeler in a preparatory tone.

"What?" asked Henry, recognizing the gravity of the moment.

"David Hix with TWRA has asked for my help. The little boy said something about a hairy creature of some sort attacking his father. Yesterday they found some large footprints they haven't been able to identify. I'm going to take a look at it. I'm leaving here in just a few minutes."

"Damn," said Henry, stunned at the new developments. "I wish I could go."

"It's best that you don't. I hear your buddy, the developer - what's his name? MacFarland? - is haranguing the investigators, trying to keep everything quiet. That could cause trouble with you and your boss," said Wheeler.

"But Mr. Wheeler, a man has died. Maybe I could offer some new insight that would help them figure out what happened," interjected Henry.

"And you will. I'd like for you to talk with David Hix sometime. He is the TWRA officer helping in the investigation. Hopefully today I can get a feel for the sheriff down there. If he's receptive to the possibility maybe we can share your story with him too."

"My God," said Henry.

"I know," said Wheeler. "I feel like we're on the verge of bringing something new, exciting, and now, terrifying to the world."

Chapter 16

Wheeler arrived at the Ridgeline Bar & Grill at one o'clock Tuesday afternoon and was met by David Hix. They rode together in Hix's large white government owned pickup truck to the turnout at the end of the logging road that provided access to Yonah Ridge and the scene of the Thurmond Raines attack. By this point the Lytle County Sheriff's Department had deployed a two passenger all-terrain vehicle to the scene to allow for easier access.

Hix parked the ATV at the top of the ridge near the deer stand. "We need to walk from here," he said. "You'll see why in a minute." Wheeler followed Hix down a narrow, even more overgrown spur of the logging road. The ground was still wet and squished beneath their feet from the rain of the previous day. After a few minutes of shuffling through the mud and pushing back what small branches had not yet been cleared by a machete they stopped at a strip of sandy mud. In it were a procession of six tracks. Four of the tracks were partial but two of them were quite clear. Unlike the traditional large human-like footprint that popular culture has associated with Bigfoot, these tracks looked more like a very large human hand, with the thumb projecting at an oblique angle toward the inside of the step rather than forward like a toe.

"Well I'll be," said Wheeler amazed, stroking his hand across his mouth and chin. "Do you mind if I take a picture?" he asked.

"No, that's fine," said Hix. "But please don't post it anywhere," he admonished.

"Of course not," said Wheeler pulling out his phone and snapping several shots from various angles. Looking at the tracks from a squatting position he asked, "Have you measured them?"

"Yes. The largest one measures sixteen and a half inches," replied Hix. "That's the one I took the cast of."

"Who all has seen these?" asked Wheeler.

"Just Sheriff Case and one his deputies. And of course, you and me. The sheriff has told Jim Finney about them as well. He's the county executive," replied Hix.

"David, you're a wildlife biologist. You know as well as I do that this isn't a bear. It isn't anything we think of as living around here," said Wheeler, earnestly.

"I agree. The closest thing I can think of is some sort of, of ape or something," said Hix, at a loss for words, still having a hard time believing the situation.

"A pongid ape," said Wheeler. "Like an orangutan. That's what those tracks look like." He looked around at the gray winter forest around him taking in the whole scene. "David, you said you had found some strands of hair. Would you mind letting me have just one of them?"

"I guess not. Like we discussed I'm taking them to the TBI [Tennessee Bureau of Investigation] lab tomorrow for a DNA test," said Hix wondering what else Wheeler would do with one of the hairs.

"Right and that will be a good test to figure out if this creature has that virus. But I can do a physical inspection of the hair at home, under a microscope and look for some physiological clues as to what we might be dealing with."

"Sure. I'll put one in a vial for you when we get back to my truck."

At this time Deputy Chumley walked up. He was agitated that Hix had brought someone to the scene.

"Who is this?" Chumley asked hotly of Hix.

"He's someone who might can help us. Joseph Wheeler. He's with the Tennessee Department of Environment and Conservation," answered Hix, a bit dismissive of the young deputy

and evading the fact that Wheeler's position within the department
had absolutely nothing to do with the investigation.

"Oh," said Chumley, partially relaxing. "Mr. MacFarland is on
his way. He wanted to see where the attack took place. I was just
making sure the tracks were still visible because Finney said he'll
probably have some questions."

"As we all do," replied Hix.

A moment later a commotion was heard sloshing through the
mud toward them. "Goddammit its slick," barked a manly voice
marked by erudition, with an inflection that broadened vowels and
left the details of enunciation to linger in nuance, with a cadence
more Southern than country. A few steps later and MacFarland,
Executive Finney, and Sheriff Case came around a clump of
mountain laurel and saw Hix and Wheeler, whom they had not
been expecting. Seeing the others present MacFarland noted,
"Well, I see you've called out the welcoming committee."

"Mr. MacFarland, this is David Hix with TWRA," said Finney,
introducing them. "And I don't believe I've had the pleasure of
meeting you yet," said Finney, turning to Wheeler.

"This is Joseph Wheeler with TDEC," said Hix.

"TDEC?" asked MacFarland, his suspicions piqued.

"Yes, that's right," said Wheeler, relishing the implications
invoked by his agency, amused at their utter irrelevancy.

"I hear your people are interested in turning this area into a
park?" lead MacFarland.

"That idea has been discussed. There is a beautiful waterfall on
this property, a little ways from here. By foot that is. You would
have to drive several miles to get there by road," said Wheeler,
playing with MacFarland's anxieties over this issue.

"Interesting. I'll have to see it sometime," said MacFarland,
ready to drop the issue until he could talk to Finney and Case in
private. "Mr. Hix, I hear there are some tracks up here that you

and Sheriff Case have some questions about?" MacFarland asked, redirecting the conversation and turning to Hix.

"Yes, they're actually right over here," said Hix, taking a few steps forward on the trail. "These tracks are highly unusual and they have me stumped. That is why I invited Mr. Wheeler out here to have a look at them," he added, trying to ease the tension that had already built between the Developer and the Conservationist."

"Well, you're a man who knows wildlife Mr. Hix. What do you think they are?" asked MacFarland.

"I know what they're not," said Hix. "They're not a man or a bear or a mountain lion. "

MacFarland looked at him incredulous, with an obvious disdain for the analytical reasoning of scientific deduction. "And what do these tracks have to do with the murder of the deer hunter?" This question made everyone uneasy. This was the moment. Finney shifted, thinking of a diplomatic way to broach the subject. Case's mind raced around ways to protect his credibility, and Chumley stood silent, an adolescent as it were quelled by the gravitas of the more mature men. Finally, Wheeler spoke up.

"Mr. MacFarland, these tracks belong to an upright, anthropoid. An ape if you will," he stated with confident resolve in his voice.

"An ape?" said MacFarland, with a sneer in his voice. "Whoever heard of such a thing in Tennessee?"

Wheeler remained steady. "Mr. MacFarland the tracks speak for themselves."

MacFarland abruptly turned to Case. "You're telling me the best answer your department can come up with is that that man was killed by Bigfoot? Is that the best you can do sheriff?" snarled MacFarland, already seeing the implications of such a story in his mind.

"Thurmond Raines, that was his name," said Case, growing impatient with MacFarland's condescending attitude. "He suffered a violent attack that didn't involve any weapons. Whatever it was that killed him was a powerful creature." Case went on, "We haven't found any human prints, no bear prints, nothing to lead us in any other direction. Now I can understand your doubts, but this is as close to a lead as we have."

"Well, I've heard it all now," said MacFarland throwing his hands up in the air with dramatic flair. "And what do you make of all this?" he asked, wheeling around to Finney who had remained silent thus far.

"I trust Sheriff Case and Officer. Hix. Mr. MacFarland, there is more to this story," said Finney, a bureaucratic type man, not weak, but one who has to dig deep to find resolve. "Sheriff, please tell Mr. MacFarland about what Wesley Raines had to say."

"Wesley Raines, Thurmond Raines son who was out here with him when the attack occurred, woke up last night after his sedative wore off. He was disoriented and terrified. His mother said he kept saying something about a large hairy monster attacking his father. His mother asked what he looked like and the boy told her he looked like a red gorilla," said Case, sighing as he finished, resigned to the fact that MacFarland would not be swayed by Wesley Raines account of the incident. And he was correct.

"That is the rambling of a scared child," ranted MacFarland. "He had probably just woken up from a bad dream. He obviously saw something terrible happen out here and that is how his brain processed it."

At this point Wheeler spoke up, irritated by what he perceived as MacFarland's bullying of community leaders who he knew needed his money. "Mr. MacFarland, is it incomprehensible to you that Thurmond Raines' violent death, his little boy's eyewitness account, and these tracks all combine to make a strong case for some creature not yet known to science being the culprit here?”

“Mr. Wheeler, I am interested in finding out what happened. If someone murdered Mr. Raines then we need to find whoever did it. If he was killed by a wild animal then we must track it down and kill it. Mr. Raines’ family and this community needs closure,” said MacFarland, a bit self-righteously.

“And you don’t want anything to stand in the way of your land grab, do you Mr. MacFarland?” barked Wheeler. “I’m sure these gentlemen are doing the best they can.”

MacFarland, backing down a bit said, “Mr. Wheeler, I believe that is one point we can agree on.” Turning to Finney and Case he said, “Mr. Finney, sheriff, thank you for showing me the location and the tracks. I can only hope your investigation goes forward smoothly from here and your community can find some closure to this tragic incident.” He looked up and noted the clouds and fading light. “It’s getting dark on us. I suppose we need to be heading back.”

Hix spoke up to Case, “Wayne, ya’ll go ahead and take the ATV down. Joe and I don’t mind walking.”

“Thank you,” said Case. “There’s only room for two.” Turning to Finney, “Jimmy why don’t you and Mr. MacFarland take the ATV.”

“Thanks Wayne. I think Mr. MacFarland and I both forgot to wear a sturdy pair of shoes so that will save us some ankle twisting.”

Finney and MacFarland rode off on the ATV as the other men walked down the logging road behind them. Chumley, who had been silent the whole time finally chimed up. “Sheriff, do you mind if I tell Mr. Wheeler about what happened out at Jim Tyree’s house a few weeks ago?”

“Yeah, go ahead Chris. That’s fine” said Case.

"What happened son?" asked Wheeler in a fatherly voice.

"Well, I got dispatched to go out to Jim Tyree's place back at the end of October. He lives on the other side of the ridge from here. It was Halloween night. He said he had seen a peeping tom on his property."

"A peeping tom?" exclaimed Wheeler. "I haven't heard that term in awhile."

"Yeah. He said that he heard his neighbor's dogs barking then he said he felt somebody rubbing up against his trailer."

"That would have to be somebody heavy to feel them rubbing up on a house trailer," reasoned Wheeler.

"That's what he said," continued Chumley. "He walked outside but didn't see anybody. He went back to bed and felt it again. He said he felt like someone was watching him. That's when he got up and pulled back the blinds on the window and he said a large hairy man was staring back at him. He thought it might have been his ex-brother-in-law, they've had some trouble."

"Did he give you any description other than *hairy*?" asked Wheeler.

"Not really," replied Chumley. "He just said hairy. But he did say there was something wild about it, its eyes. He couldn't really put his finger on it. Then he said it got scared and ran away when he screamed. I guess whatever it was, was as scared as Jim had been."

"Does anyone else know about this incident?" asked Wheeler.

"I mentioned it to Finney this morning," said Case. "I'd rather not read too much into it because Jim Tyree has had a lot of trouble with his brother-in-law. Bad blood there. It being Halloween night and all it's really likely it was him messing with Jim, trying to intimidate him" said Case, obviously wanting to keep the two cases separate.

98

"Well I'm glad you told me about it anyway," said Wheeler. "Given the proximity to our location and the uncertainty this Mr. Tyree expressed I'd say he may have had an encounter with our creature."

The four men sloshed down the trail for a moment in the gloaming light of the darkening forest. Suddenly Sheriff Case spoke up, "So what do we do now Mr. Wheeler? You've seen the tracks, you've heard what Wesley Raines described. Where do we go from here?" He sounded exasperated.

"Sheriff, I really don't know. I know what to do from the point of view of a researcher. I'd put out the word inviting people all over the county to describe any encounters they may have had or any encounters they may have heard their friends or family talk about. These sightings aren't a new phenomenon."

"They're not? I thought all this Bigfoot business got started in the fifties or sixties?" asked Hix.

"No siree," said Wheeler. With the dark coming on he started feeling excited as if he were about to tell a ghost story around a campfire. "Just eighty miles or so north of here in Kentucky there is a place called Monkey Cave Holler," he stated, the hard "r" of *hollow* being his natural pronunciation of the word.

"Do you know how it got that name?" asked Chumley.

"Yes, apparently there was a tribe of apes of some sort used to live up there. On our website one investigator wrote about an interview he did years ago with an old-timer who claimed to have seen the last one after it had been killed. That would have been back in the early 1900's. I'm sure the person telling the story is long dead by now if he was a little boy back then, old enough to remember it."

"You make a compelling argument Mr. Wheeler but I'm afraid dealing with the public isn't as analytical as scientific research," said Case, sounding exhausted.

"No sheriff, my job too has taught me that public relations is an art. An imperfect one at that," replied Wheeler. It was dark by the time they reached their vehicles at the bottom of the logging road. Deep in the woods, back up on the ridge coyotes yipped in a frenzied orgy of sound, wild ghost dogs singing their haunted song to the night.

Chapter 17

Henry was stirring a pot of cheap spaghetti sauce when his phone rang. He shook the spoon to free it of the dripping, thin liquid then laid it down and answered his phone. "Hello."

"Henry, its Joseph. I'm not interrupting anything am I?"

"No, not at all," said Henry, with a fleeting forlornness that there was in fact nothing in his life to interrupt once the work day was over.

"Good. I'm just getting back from my trip over to Lytle County."

"Yeah, how did it go?" asked Henry. "Did you find anything interesting?"

"You might say that," Wheeler coyly replied.

"Well?"

"I know it's getting later but can you come over to my house this evening?"

"Sure," said Henry, with a dismissive glance at the spaghetti sauce. "You live down in Oak Hills, right?"

"I do. I'll text you my address. What do you say, meet me in about forty-five minutes?"

"Sounds perfect," said Henry.

***

At 7:30 p.m. Henry pulled his beat-up green pickup into the drive of an older, ranch style brick home that sat a hundred feet off the road. Three large silver maples stood in the front yard. He walked up to the concrete portico past thirty-year-old, overgrown boxwoods and rang the doorbell. Wheeler immediately answered, "Come in, come in," shaking Henry's hand as he walked through the door. Wheeler led him down a hallway past rooms of nice furniture that were in perfect order. But the neatness of the rooms seemed to be more a result of lack of use rather than a conscious effort to keep everything tidy. "If you have a little time we can order a pizza," suggested Wheeler.

"That would be awesome but don't go to any special trouble just for me," said Henry modestly.

"Nonsense, I was going to have one anyway," said Wheeler matter-of-factly. "What do you like on yours?"

"Anything you get will be fine," said Henry. "From anchovies to artichoke hearts, I like it all."

"Fine then. I was hoping you liked anchovies. I'll order a supreme and when it gets here I'll open a can and throw the pizza in the oven for five minutes to heat them up." Wheeler led Henry to his study and turned on a corner lamp. Henry looked around the room while Wheeler ordered the pizza. A map of North America adorned the wall. Next to it was a map of Tennessee. Push pins were embedded in it at different points where Wheeler had collected reports of bigfoot sightings. A large book case covered half of one wall from the floor nearly to the ceiling. In the center of the room sat a large desk that held a computer with a large monitor. A good binocular microscope sat to one side. "This is my man cave," said Wheeler after he had finished ordering the pizza. "Some old men want woodshops or garages to restore old cars in. I have my cryptozoology research area."

"This is really cool," said Henry, who felt the whole house was comfortable and spacious. So different from his cramped efficiency apartment. He noticed a mandolin hanging on the wall. "I didn't know you played mandolin?" said Henry, nodding at the instrument.

"Yeah, I've been picking on it here and there for forty years," replied Wheeler.

"Do you mind?" asked Henry, gesturing toward the instrument.

"No, go right ahead," said Wheeler. "Are you a picker?"

"I'm a hunt and pecker," said Henry taking down the instrument. He plucked around on a few chords and filled some runs of notes in between. "This is a nice mandolin, sounds good" he said.

"You do a good job on that thing," said Wheeler.

"I've played guitar and mandolin off and on since I was about twelve or thirteen. Just something I picked up. Kind of like surveying," said Henry bashfully.

"We'll pick a little bit next time you come over," said Wheeler, ready to move on to the investigation. He pulled out his phone and brought up the pictures of the tracks. "Here's something you might be interested in," he said, passing Henry the phone.

Henry looked at the pictures, swiping the screen to zoom in and out. "Wow! These tracks were at the site of the attack?" he asked.

"Yes, very close by."

"How far were they from where I took you the other day?"

"I'm not too sure," said Wheeler. "We took a different way in today but it is definitely in the same area. I'd say within a mile or so."

"So, these aren't what I've always thought of as classic 'bigfoot' tracks," said Henry. "You know, the ones that look like a human foot, but a lot bigger."

"No, they don't look like that and that's one reason these tracks are so interesting," said Wheeler. He looked at the phone with Henry. Pointing at the screen he went on, "See what we would think of as the big toe, here?" he asked.

"Yes," said Henry following the discussion.

"That looks a lot like a thumb doesn't it? The way it sticks out to the side like that," said Wheeler.

"Yes."

"That's because the creature I believe we're looking for isn't a classic bigfoot like people think of when they think of bigfoot sightings out in California and the Pacific Northwest."

"Then what is it?" asked Henry, having never realized there was more than one kind of North American ape.

"Henry what we have here is a pongid ape. Like gorillas, chimps, and orangutans. The shape of that tarsal, the way it's jointed is one characteristic that sets them apart from humans."

"So, are you saying what I saw and whatever left these tracks might be an animal that escaped from a private zoo or something?" asked Henry, faintly disappointed that there might be a more mundane explanation to his encounter.

"That is always a possibility, you and I both know true science rules out the likelihood of something, never outright denies the possibility. But sightings of such animals have happened many, many times, almost always in the East. I've interviewed country people who called them wood-boogers. Quite different from what people think of when they speak about a Bigfoot like the on the Patterson-Gimlin film. There are at least two species of apes native to North America," said Wheeler.

"But I just don't understand how they've never been seen and scientifically documented," said Henry, almost calling his own encounter into question.

"Who says they haven't Henry?" asked Wheeler playing the role of the mentor. "You told me what you saw didn't you?"

"Yes, but-"

"I've documented these tracks with a photo and David Hix took a cast of one them. That's documentation isn't it?" asked Wheeler.

"Yes."

"And there are a handful of place names spread across the country, in remote areas. Names like Ape Canyon and Monkey Cave Holler. Just like Buffalo Valley or the Buffalo River here in Tennessee. Places named after something that used to live there," said Wheeler, persuasively.

"Yeah, I see your point," said Henry, understanding.

"And look at this," said Wheeler, pulling the vial containing the hair David Hix had given him out of his pocket. "This hair came from the site of the attack. Doesn't look much like a deer or coyote hair does it?" asked Wheeler, handing the vial to Henry.

"No, it's way too long," said Henry, inspecting the vial.

"Exactly," agreed Wheeler. "You're observing from the point of view of common sense. But you remember what I say about common sense -"

"Common sense is often common misconception," said Henry, reciting Wheeler's quote from a previous conversation.

"That's right," said Wheeler. "So, let us look at this hair scientifically," he said, taking the vial, walking to the desk and setting up the microscope. Using the tweezers of his Swiss Army knife he carefully removed the hair from the vial and placed it on a slide then gently laid a cover slip over it. Then turning to Henry, who watched on with rapt attention, he said, "Now Henry, we've decided this hair isn't from a cow or deer or anything we can think of. Right?"

"Right, unless it's from a person."

"That's right. And what do humans and chimps, one of the pongid apes, have in common?"

"Uh, opposable thumbs?" said Henry, trying to read Wheeler's mind.

"Yes, that's correct. But more importantly humans and chimps share about 98% of the same DNA. Therefore, I would expect this hair to look a lot like human hair."

"I think it already does," said Henry.

"Yes, but let's go beyond an overall impression and get to the meat of the matter." Wheeler focused the lens on the hair. "Okay. What do you see?" asked Wheeler moving over, inviting Henry to have a look.

"Wow, I feel like I'm at work," said Henry, referring to the similarity between looking through a microscope and looking through a surveying instrument, both of which bring hidden details, invisible details, into sharp focus. "It's amazing to see pits in a strand of hair. This really brings out the 3-D structure," said Henry, slightly turning the knob to adjust the focus in and out. "The hair looks distinctly redder than it did to my naked eye. I see small flecks of something-"

"That's melanin granules. They give it the color," said Wheeler knowingly. "Do you see an inner core that looks hollow?" Wheeler lead. Henry looked hard for the core.

"No, I don't see anything I would describe as that."

"That's right. Unlike most mammals, human hair and ape hair doesn't contain a well-defined medulla."

"But how do we know this isn't human hair?" asked Henry, baffled.

"We don't. But with the combined evidence of the prints and the sightings and the little boy - I told you he had talked, didn't I?" asked Wheeler, interrupting his own line of reasoning.

"Yes," replied Henry. "You said he had said something about a hairy monster."

"Well Henry, it seems to me that the evidence is there to support the theory that Thurmond Raines was attacked by either a person or a hominid, perhaps unknown to science. But with you

106

and that other fella both having a visual encounter in the area, the tracks, and the only eyewitness present saying his father was attacked by a hairy "monster" you can guess which way I'm leaning," declared Wheeler.

"I agree with you," said Henry. "But what about the people investigating the incident? What do they think?"

"David Hix, the TWRA officer who called me, is 100% in agreement. I think the sheriff and county executive are inclined to agree as well. But they have the public to deal with and blaming a man's death on Bigfoot," at this Wheeler hooked his fingers to imply air quotes, "isn't an easy sell for law enforcement. They're in a tough spot," he said, empathetically.

"So what next?" asked Henry.

"I suppose we'll continue to investigate the incident quietly, looking for incontrovertible evidence. And in the meantime, let's hope nobody else gets hurt." The moment was interrupted by the three chimes of a door bell. "There's our pizza," said Wheeler, giving Henry an affectionate pat on the shoulder.

Chapter 18

Chip Greenfield and Lauren Delorenzo were friends and occasional lovers who shared a mutual passion for the outdoors. They were both English majors at the university in Murfreesboro. Their fine art sensibilities had inculcated in them a love for photography, film, and performance art. The one dark side in their relationship was the fact that Lauren was married. Her husband, Michael, was currently in Guatemala working with a non-profit that attempted to build business relationships with local villagers. Ideally the organization would trade the villagers a fair wage in return for authentic hand-woven rugs and masks featuring hand carved images of Quetzalcoatl. These items would then be sold to arm-chair travelers in the United States. But Michael would be back in town in a few days to celebrate the long Thanksgiving weekend. That's why Chip and Lauren had decided to take a pre-Thanksgiving camping trip to film themselves reading poetry out in a splendid natural setting and do whatever it took to ease the tensions that would be brought on by the upcoming holiday.

Chip and Lauren had at first thought of spending the night in a cabin at the resort park of Fall Creek Falls but they decided against it, instead wanting to experience something new, something where they would not be interrupted by the presence of others. Having heard about Virgin Falls from a friend, they went online and found the directions. They had arrived at noon, parking on the shoulder where Wheeler and Henry had parked when they had visited the waterfall at the end of October. Being students lured from distant hometowns by a major university, Chip from west Tennessee, Lauren from Massachusetts, they paid little attention to local news and neither had heard about the attack on Thurmond Raines that had occurred just six days before across the ridge from where they now entered the woods.

The day was overcast but pretty, the light perfect for photography. After an hour of walking they stopped in front of a large cave where Lauren pulled out a lunch of cheese, triscuits, and apples from her backpack. Chip pulled a bottle of pinot noir from his. He uncorked it with his Swiss Army knife and passed it to Lauren to sample the first sip. "Mmmmm...that's good," she said, indulging in the rich sweetness of the wine, swishing it around in her mouth to get the texture of it, rolling her tongue and making a sucking sound to discover the hidden flavors. She handed the bottle back to Chip. He took a swig, imitating Lauren's tasting techniques.

"Ummm, it is tasty," he agreed, inwardly knowing that as long as it was wet and would give him a buzz, he was going to like it anyway. They lingered over their cheese and crackers and occasionally took slow bites of sliced apples. After half the bottle of wine was gone Lauren stood up and said she was ready to recite a poem. Looking around to make sure they were alone, she untied her boots then stood up and slipped off her pants and stripped off her shirt. She stepped into a pair of brown sandals, picked up a white sheet, and then, wearing just her bra and panties, she ran down to the cave and hopped across some small boulders that littered the creek at the mouth of the cave. She wrapped the sheet around her ample breasts and torso, toga fashion, and scouted for a good spot to stand. As she did this Chip unpacked his camera, a digital SLR that also shot high quality video. He checked the light and re-checked it again. He had Lauren perform some test recitations to check the audio quality. "Audio is pretty good," he said. "If we want better we can always overdub later." He fiddled with the camera a moment more. "Okay, I like the way you're framed. Start reciting whenever you're ready."

Lauren looked up into the canopy of bare poplar branches and dark needled hemlock and took a deep breath. Then she stared ahead, focusing on a large buckeye, though she did not know that was what the tree was called. She began to recite a poem, composing it on the spot:

> *As time in nature's boughs*
> *The water of life given*
> *The nature of my life is revealed*
> *A hell on earth or heaven*
> *When bicameral desire is riven*
> *And both my loves allowed*
> *The sanctity of my true love is heaven*
> *My lover's carnal pleasure is hell*

As she spoke the last lines she cast her gaze down toward the water, her blue eyes open wide, her thin lips pinched into a slightly too-tight effort at a pout, to give the effect of deep thought and reflection.

"Aaaaaand CUT!" said Chip. "That was great."

"Are you sure my accent was right?" asked Lauren looking up from her impromptu stage, the cave's gaping maw behind her.

"Yeah, it was perfect," reassured Chip. He looked up at the gray sky through the canopy. "We probably need to get on to the waterfall," he said. "We don't want to run out of light."

"Okay. I'm ready to put some clothes back on," said Lauren, hugging her arms close to her body and affecting a shiver. "It's cold out here when you're only wearing a toga."

A few minutes after they began walking the trail turned to the left and they began a sharp descent into a hollow. The decaying leaves of umbrella magnolia, ten inches wide and nearly two feet long, made an unsightly white mess on the otherwise varying shades of brown of the forest floor. As Chip turned and took Lauren's hand to steady her while going down a steep embankment

110

they heard two loud knocks come from deep in the woods. It was like someone had hit the trunk of a tree with a baseball bat. "What was that?" asked Laura.

"I heard it too," said Chip. "It sounded like wood on wood. A branch may have fallen out of a tree." They thought nothing more of it and continued walking another half hour. Coming around the shoulder of a small hill, they entered the hollow and heard the sonorous white noise of falling water up ahead.

"Ohhh, I bet that's it," said Lauren, excited.

"Yeah it must be," said Chip. "The directions said it was about a mile and a half in. I bet we've come that far." They walked deeper into the hollow and after a few minutes stood before a thick veil of falling water, a refreshing sheet in liquid motion, tumbling with the force of gravity; an element of the earth in harmonious play with the forces that had shaped it, trickling through crevices and evaporating into the clouds above, where it would rain down again, repeating the cycle, all the while cutting deeper and deeper into the bedrock of the earth, slowly revealing the mysteries below.

Chip and Lauren stood before the waterfall amazed, baptized in the spray from its booming deluge. "It's so beautiful," cried Lauren, with a flush of emotion, overcome by the awesome spectacle.

"It's amazing," agreed Chip. "So powerful. I'm glad we're here after a good rain." He scanned the amphitheater around the waterfall. "It is so strange. Look down there," he said, putting his arm around Lauren's shoulder and pointing to a small, perhaps six foot, opening cradled between a rim a large boulders. "It's like the water just disappears underground."

"Yes, it's lovely, sublime, even a little creepy," she giggled over the boom of the diluvian spectacle.

"Let's scout around for a place to camp and drop our gear then we'll get some footage of you in front of the falls," said Chip. They followed the hillside around toward the head of the hollow. Walking a little ways up toward the crest of the hill, they found a level spot that afforded a good view of the waterfall. Chip slid the heavy pack off his back. "I'll go ahead and set up the tent right now. It won't take any time at all. Then we'll have the rest of the daylight to film."

"Sounds good," said Lauren. "I'll go ahead and get changed." With this she once again slipped off her jeans and shirt. She walked around the ridge to the waterfall carrying the white sheet in her hand. As she walked, she heard the distinctive hoot of an owl. She stopped and cocked her head, pulling her shoulder length dark brown hair back around her ear to better listen. She heard the hoot again. Slightly disconcerted by the hoot and the wilderness around her she turned back toward Chip and yelled, "Chip, did you hear that?"

"Hear what?" he asked, sliding the pole that supported the tent through the grommets that held it.

"That owl," she replied.

He stopped what he was doing and craned his ear toward the woods. "No," he said. I don't hear anything.

"No big deal," said Lauren, continuing to walk. "I just didn't know there were owls out in the daytime." Chip had resumed his work of putting up the tent, unable to hear Lauren over the roar of the falls.

Ten minutes later she was in place, clad in the toga. Chip, with his camera in hand, moved about experimenting with different ways of framing her. He suddenly realized that nothing she said was going to be picked up over the din of the waterfall. "Hey, I won't be able to hear you," he yelled.

"What?" Lauren yelled back.

"Exactly." Pointing at the camera Chip said, "I'm just going to take a few pictures right now." Still not quite understanding what

Chip was saying, Lauren watched him for a moment then realized he was photographing her. She turned her head in different directions and held up her arms as if making an offering to the waterfall. Chip clicked away on the other side of the narrow hollow. Then she had an idea. Smiling, she reached behind her back and untied the toga. She took off her bra and panties and stood nude in front of the sheet of falling water. Chip was loving it, excited, feeling the tingle of an erection at the sight of Lauren's round, ivory white breasts and the dark triangle of pubic hair. But this was work no matter how titillating. He continued to photograph as Lauren posed like a Druid princess in an enchanted forest of dreams. He slowly worked his way around the hillside, finding new perspectives as Lauren moved around, peering out from behind dark old growth hemlocks and, somewhat unflatteringly, bent herself over a boulder the size of a sofa.

After a few minutes Chip made his way around to where Lauren stood. She was cold now, wet with the spray from Virgin Falls. Chip pulled her to him, enveloping her in his warm arms. He cupped his hands around her goose-bumped bottom. They kissed. "Oh, I hate to say it, but you should get dressed and warm up before it gets dark out," said Chip, reluctantly letting Lauren go.

"I am cold and wet. But I bet we got some great pictures," she teased.

"Yes. Wonderful. We can look through them later on after it gets dark." They walked back around the hillside to where Lauren had left her clothes. She dressed and they walked back around toward the waterfall, this time angling their way up the hill to the top of the falls. There they found the cave from which the falls emerged. They walked up to the mouth of it, smelling the sharp, rust and ozone smell of stone and water emanating from deep in the limestone earth. A steady breeze blew out of the cave, the air about the same temperature as the outside air. In summer it would have provided a refreshing coolness in contrast to the summer heat, but for now the temperature inside the cave was about the same as that outside it.

"Caves are so spooky," said Lauren, apprehensive but at the same time adventurous enough to take the first step into the mouth of the cave.

"Yes, they are. Such strange features on the land. It feels sort of like peering into your own soul when you think about it. Something dark and unknown, something you only get to explore in special moments," said Chip.

"Something our senses are not quite equipped to handle," agreed Lauren.

"The mystery of the cave. Just like Plato wrote about. If our lives were lived from within the darkness of a cave, what horror and wonder would the sunlit world outside hold for us?" asked Chip, rhetorically. He stepped on a small rock that was poorly balanced on a pebble and stumbled as it gave way beneath him. He splashed loudly in the four-inch-deep water, trying to regain his balance. 'Shit!" he exclaimed. "Now my boots are soaked!"

The commotion of Chip's misstep disturbed something deep within the cave. Just as Chip had stumbled over a rock and splashed heavily in the water to regain his balance, the sound of footsteps sloshing hurriedly through the subterranean creek came from somewhere deep in the cave. At the same time the constant cool breeze that blew from deep within now carried a curious odor, like that of a wet dog, mixed together with the smell of earth and forest. "Oh my god, what was that?" asked Lauren, startled by the sound, and the odor indicating the presence of some animal in the cave.

"I don't know," said Chip, "but I bet we're in the lair of a wild animal of some sort," he said, then squinting his eyes and turning back to Lauren he said, "a BEAR!" and made a growl and grabbed her, eliciting a squeal and giggle from her yielding body. He looked back at the cave entrance. "We'd better get out of here," he said. "I left our flashlight in my backpack. I don't want it to get dark on us."

"You don't?" said Lauren, pulling Chip's face close to her. "I do. I'm ready for the night. The night belongs to lovers," she said, kissing him, squeezing the back of his neck and rubbing her hand across his shoulders.

On the way back to their camp Chip and Lauren utilized the remaining daylight to gather firewood. With the sun setting behind the ridge the temperature was dropping and, despite the pleasant temperatures of the day, it promised to be a chilly, if not cold night. Back at camp Chip tore paper into strips and snapped twigs and laid them on top of the paper. Lauren returned with a last bundle of sticks to fuel their small fire.

She opened the second bottle of wine. She took a swig from the bottle and passed it to Chip, who had lit a cigarette and watched his fire to see if the little flame he had got started was going to last. "I'm starved," she said, fumbling through her pack.

"Me too," said Chip. "That was a pretty good hike."

Lauren pulled a can of chili out of the pack and the box of crackers from earlier. Digging into Chip's pack, she pulled out a small plastic cylinder which held a triangular gas burner. Exercising great care, she balanced the can of chili on the tripod surface of the burner and waited for it to heat up. "It's been a good day," she said.

"I've enjoyed it," replied Chip.

"I'm going to miss you next weekend," said Lauren, forlornly.

"You'll see your husband," said Chip, matter-of-factly.

"That's over," she said. "I love him, but it's over."

"Yeah, sometimes distance just doesn't work out."

"He cheated on me last time he went out of town," she said. "It was with a girl from the Peace Corps. I told you about that, right?"

"You mentioned it but you know I've never liked discussing him. When you're with me I want it to just be us," said Chip, patting her knee, knowing Lauren was either lying or delusional regarding her husband's supposed infidelity.

"Me too," she said with a soft smile. "Soul mates."

They ate their dinner and crawled into their sleeping bags inside the tent. Though they had intended to read, the sounds of tickles and giggling soon spilled out of the tent to fill the human void in the darkness.

"Whoo Wh-Whoo Whoo Wh-Whoo," called a voice in the night.

"Listen," said Lauren, cocking her head toward the sound. "Hear it?"

"What?" asked Chip, excited, aroused, more interested in wild sex than wildlife.

"It's the owl again."

"Whoo Wh-Whoo Whoo Wh-Whoo," came the call again.

"Yeah I hear it," said Chip, rolling back over toward Lauren and roughly kissing her shoulder.

"Oh, you have a one track mind," she said, laughing, running her hand up his thigh.

"You can't blame me," he cooed, "It's all your fault." Suddenly they heard two loud knocks, the sound of a large stick hitting the trunk of a tree.

"Holy shit," exclaimed Chip. "What was that?" he asked, slipping on his underwear, hurriedly reaching for his pants. They heard the knocking sound again and then twigs snapping, coming closer. Something was walking towards them through the forest. Chip fumbled for the flashlight and crawled out of the tent. "Who's out there?" he yelled into the night. The sound of the swishing branches stopped. The darkness was heavy with silence. A foul odor, the similar but more rancid than the one they had smelled in the cave, came to Chip's nostrils on a light breeze.

"Chip, what is it?" asked Lauren from inside the tent, a stutter in her voice.

"I don't know," he said, calming a bit. "There's that smell again. I think it's whatever was inside the cave. It's just an animal we startled. Everything's going to be okay," he said, turning off the flashlight and kneeling down to crawl back into the tent.

"I'm afraid," cried Lauren, wrapping her arms around Chip as he returned to his sleeping bag.

"AAAAAAARRRRRRRRRRRR!" came a guttural roar that shook the tent. Just as the roar subsided a stick, which had been flung from a distance, crashed through the branches above and fell heavily on the ground, just missing the tent.

"Alright, fuck this!" yelled Chip, jumping back outside the tent. "What the fuck do you want?" he screamed into the darkness.

The echo of his scream faded and for a moment there was only silence, save the sound of the falling water. And then suddenly there was the crashing and cracking sound of something running through the brush. Chip wheeled around but was met by the impact of a devastating blow before he ever had a chance to see the broad shoulders or heavy, hairy arm. He fell against a tree as the powerful hand grabbed him, flinging him down to the ground where the point of a rock cracked through his occipital lobe and the frames of Chip's movie went out of focus, flickered, then faded to black forever.

The creature stood over Chip's smashed body for a moment, waiting for it to move. Sensing that he had killed the intruder, he leaned back his head and let out a blood curdling, howling roar that reverberated throughout the amphitheater of the gorge. All the while Lauren huddled in the tent, sobbing, shaking, urinating at the sound of the howl. She leaned farther and farther into the soft wall of the tent, her animal brain telling her a small, close place was safe while her reasoning human brain would have told her the thin fabric afforded no protection. But Lauren was running on instinct now.

The creature sniffed the air, turned his head at the sound of Lauren's whispered cries. She knew the creature was there. Instinct told her to be as quiet as possible but she was stressed, she was a slave to her physiology which made her weep and tremble as a means of distributing the stress so that it wouldn't cause any permanent harm. The creature turned and stepped toward the tent. Its scent was overpowering. Lauren sensed its presence, coming closer. "Chip! Chip!" she screamed to no avail. "Chip! Aaaaagggghhhh!"

The utter terror in Lauren's high-pitched scream startled the creature who stopped and stood for a moment, listening, trying to detect vibrations on the air. He roared. "AAAAAARRRRR!" After the roar subsided, he listened again, hearing Lauren's feeble mutters from inside the tent. In an explosion of motion, the creature stepped forward and grabbed the tent with his powerful hand and flung it, causing the seam to rip. Lauren partially fell out of the tent, her torso now lying on the bare ground, her legs still bound in the sleeping bag inside the tent.

The creature walked over to her, standing above her. She closed her eyes, repelled by the creature's large size, the hairy body, the grotesque, human-like face. The smell. She curled into the fetal position. The creature grabbed her roughly by the wrist, scraping her cheek in the process. He drug Lauren and the tent for perhaps ten feet across the rocky ground, eventually causing Lauren to fall completely out of the tent. She cried and screamed hysterically at first while in the creature's grasp, but then went numb, no longer fighting, no longer struggling. The creature felt the limpness of Lauren's body and stopped. He reached down and rubbed the blood on her cheek. He smelled it, then put his finger to his tongue, tasting it. He kneeled on his haunches for some time, brooding over this creature he had found. She was different from the others of her kind. He did not sense the inherent violence he had sensed in the males. He did not feel the need to establish dominance. He didn't feel threatened. He reached down and stroked her hair. Lauren mumbled at the touch, causing the creature to jump back, startled at her movement. The fact that she was not dead eased his tension and anxiety. He understood that she was not like him. He let out a soft gurgle of emotive sounds, like a dog, like the ape that he was. He lacked the brain development and facial musculature for true speech, but through his sounds one could easily differentiate between rage and tenderness, dominance and frustration.

He softly stroked Lauren's arm again as she gazed into the dark forest, eyes gleaming with tears, wide open in a blank stare. Once again, the creature moaned softly then stood up and walked away, leaving Lauren lying naked on the forest floor, the cold night surrounding her, no benevolent myth of Mother Earth to comfort or protect her.

Chapter 19

Henry awoke early on Sunday morning to the whimpers of an Aussie-mix that was a sweetheart of a dog. *Hmmmf! Hmmmf!* the dog sniffed, shoving its wet nose into Henry's face. "I know I know, I know!" said Henry, rolling out of bed. The dog - Bella - belonged to his long-time neighbors, a married couple who had gone out of town to celebrate an early Thanksgiving with family. Henry had happily agreed to look after Bella while they were gone. When a man is single and conducts most of his social interactions at work or sitting on a barstool, the presence of a dog can fill a void that he knows is there all along but he is too empty to know how to remedy.

Henry let Bella out to run around in the fenced in back yard. While the dog was outside Henry dressed and filled up a couple of water bottles. He stuffed some cheese and crackers and a stick of pepperoni into a daypack. He called Bella back to the house then walked out and started his truck. It was a chilly morning, the clear skies having let the temperature dip down to the low forties overnight. But it promised to be a nice day, sunny and around sixty, probably one of the last nice days of the year. That is why he had decided to drive out to Yonah ridge to hike back to the waterfall and, based on the evidence Wheeler had shown him, look for more traces of the creature. Henry opened the door for Bella, who effortlessly jumped up into the passenger seat. Dog Is My Co-Pilot.

Henry picked up a ham and biscuit and cup of coffee on the way out of Nashville then drove across rolling hills and the green and brown cow dotted pastures of the November landscape under a sunny blue sky. At ten o'clock he arrived at the pull out where the faint trail into Virgin Falls started. He walked through the warming, fragrant forest as thick, dried leaves of chestnut oak cracked beneath his feet. The whole time he walked he scanned the forest floor for any signs of tracks and checked the scaly bark of hickories for any long, loose red hairs. Of course, he found nothing.

This is like looking for arrowheads: when they are there, they jump out at you. You couldn't miss it, couldn't ignore it if you tried. They are all around us all the time, arrowheads litter the forest floor like beer cans in ditches along country roads. Ubiquitous. Everywhere. Just like arrowheads, so are tracks of Bigfoot, this creature you know, who you have witnessed and with whom you have shared a communion of fear. Such are the traces of his life in the forest primeval where every hope and care of his existence plays out under the sun that warms and gives hope and life to us all. The mysteries of the earth, hidden in plain sight. Sometimes awe-inspiring, sometimes awfully terrifying, when the unknown comes into conflict with the known. Which is more disconcerting? That which is completely unknown, a never considered void in the darkness of our thoughts? Or the unknown we suspect is there because of traces this amorphous entity of our fears leaves behind? Enough evidence to make someone believe, just enough of a trace to make you run through the streets shouting to the world what you have seen. Just a glimpse of the mystery that reveals itself as truth, just enough to make a true believer out of you, just enough to make the rest of the world think you're crazy.

Henry walked for an hour, looking for tracks, taking in the sights and smells of the forest as ecosystem transitioned into winter. The scurrying activity of squirrels carrying nuts and birds flitting from one berry bush to the next, all the while his internal monologue rolling along, making sense out of the sordid events that are the mundanity and complexity of life. *Where does paying bills and hoping to find the right girl and wishing I could travel a little in my life fit in with what life is all about? Things we are supposed to want out of this world that happens to others without them even having to think about it. The good life, where does it come from and why does it look so similar from one person to the next and we all have to travel, travail, down so many different roads to get there?*

Bella had run up the trail ahead of Henry. Looking up and not seeing her anywhere jarred Henry out of his reverie. "Bella!" he yelled, cupping one hands to his mouth. "Bella!"

"IIIIIIIIGGHHHHHHH!" Henry heard the shrill scream of a woman come from just up the trail. Just as the scream faded away Bella came running back down the trail toward Henry, coming to a prancing stop at his side, intelligent eyes looking straight into Henry's, waiting to see what they would do next. Henry patted Bella on the head and ran up the trail in the direction of the scream. He rounded the side of the hill to find Lauren shivering, huddled against the side of a large hemlock. She had a torn sleeping bag loosely wrapped around her shoulders. Numb and gazing off in the same blank stare as the night before, she at first did not notice Henry's presence. But once again she saw Bella running up to her and cringed yet simultaneously reached out for the dog's comforting, furry body.

"My god! What happened to you? Are you okay?" asked Henry running to the girl's side, kneeling down beside her.

"Help me," she weakly pleaded.

"Here, here," he said pulling her close to him, wrapping his arms around her cold, quivering shoulders.

Invigorated and comforted by Henry's warmth and kind touch she began to cry. "Oh my God save me, save me. Don't let it come back, don't let it come back," she sobbed, burying her head into his shoulder.

Not understanding what she was talking about Henry just held her close to him for a few minutes, "It's okay. It's okay," he said. "We're gonna get you out of here." Henry stroked the girl's knotted and frayed hair. He looked around. Behind him, about thirty feet away, he saw the feet and legs of another person. He helped the girl to her feet. Realizing she was still naked under the sleeping bag he walked her to the tent and dug out her clothes from inside. Henry inspected the man's body on the ground. He saw the pool of congealed blood and saw that the man's head had been crushed on a rock. An unsettling scenario began to take shape in Henry's mind.

"Aaaaahhhh!" the girl screamed when she saw Chip's body on the ground, the thick red blood darker than the rocks and leaves where he lay. "Get me out of here! Get me out of here!" she screamed hysterically, scaring Bella, who took refuge at Henry's side, leaning against his leg.

"I'm going to, I'm going to. I promise," said Henry. He pulled out his phone and snapped some pictures of the dead man lying on the ground and a few shots of the tent and scattered camping gear. He put his phone back in his pocket and put his arm around the girl's shoulder, she was still shivering, "Okay, okay," he said. "Let's take it easy and I'll get you out of here," he said tenderly. They slowly began walking out the trail toward the road.

Chapter 20

Sheriff Wayne Case had the dazed look of a man who had just watched a train wreck in slow motion as he hung up the phone. Another dead body out on Yonah Ridge. "I'll call Finney," he thought, just one of the many thoughts of actions and consequences which were running through his mind.

After explaining the situation to Finney, Case and Deputy Chumley got in the patrol SUV and drove out to the head of the trail where Henry had agreed to meet them. As they pulled up Case saw Lauren bedraggled and catatonic climb into an ambulance. *I have no idea how I'm going to talk to her* thought Case.

As the ambulance pulled off Henry, Case and Chumley, were joined by Luke Sudderth and Jim Gaither of the Lytle County Volunteer EMS. Just as they had done a week before, they pulled a stretcher out of the back and the five men started up the trail to where Chip Greenfield's body lay attracting the last insects of the season in the mild warmth of the sunny day. Bella ran ahead of them up the trail. Apart from Henry giving a brief synopsis of how he had come up on the girl that morning and the scattered camp site, no one said much on the hike in.

When they arrived at the body a swarm of flies had lit on the dried blood, but other than that the forest was quiet, save the eternal boom of the waterfall. Deputy Chumley took a few photos of the body and the campsite then pulled out a notebook and began writing a report, taking dictation from Sheriff Case. The EMS volunteers lifted the body. "This is near where the hunter was killed, isn't it?" asked Henry.

"Yes, fairly near here," said Case, non-committaly, unaware of Henry's role in the saga unfolding on Yonah Ridge.

"As I said on the way in, the girl kept saying something about 'don't let it come back'. What do you think *it* might be Sheriff?" asked Henry.

"I guess whatever killed this man. A bear or something," said Case, dismissive, evasive of Henry's questioning.

"With all due respect Sheriff, I think you know that's bullshit," said Henry, surprised by his own flush of emotion. "Joe Wheeler showed me the tracks you found out here." At this Case looked up, feeling threatened.

"And why would he show you that? That's official evidence," barked Case.

"Because a month before that happened, I saw one of those monsters, apes, Bigfoot, whatever you want to call it. I saw it out here! On Yonah Ridge! About a mile from here as the crow flies." Henry's outburst attracted the attention of the EMS volunteers who had the body on the stretcher and were waiting for Case and Chumley to finish up so all could lend a hand carrying the body out to the road. Case, still trying to maintain the secret, pulled Henry aside.

"Listen, don't be talking about that in front of other people around here. Now this guy here, he's not from around here, nobody knows him. But both Jim and Luke over there knew Thurmond Raines. This is personal for them and they don't want to hear about some fucking monkey killing their friend," said Case, with enough heat to get his point across.

"Then what?" asked Henry. "Are you just going to keep it under wraps for another week and let somebody else get killed? It's a holiday weekend coming up," pleaded Henry. "There'll be deer hunters, more hikers. For whatever reason, that thing has killed two people in a week. Sheriff, you can't just pretend it isn't there."

"Do you see any footprints out here?" asked Case, sarcastically. "Do you see any monkey hand prints on that man's body? Why the hell are you so sure an ape killed these people?"

"Because of what the girl said. And what the little boy said." Case turned around at the mention of Wesley Raines' nightmare at the hospital. "Sheriff, Mr. Wheeler told me about that too."

"Your friend Mr. Wheeler talks too much," said Case, walking brusquely past Henry, back toward the body.

"So, what are we going to do about it Sheriff?" challenged Henry.

"I don't know. But right now we're going to carry this man's body out of the woods and notify his family. I'd appreciate your help with the stretcher." Henry looked down, kicked at the ground then walked over and helped hoist the stretcher. Bella followed tiredly behind, having already had a long day.

Chapter 21

On the drive back to Nashville Henry called Wheeler to discuss the events of the day. Wheeler was shocked and intrigued. But, more and more, he was angry that Sheriff Case seemed so reluctant to face the truth of the source of the attacks and be honest with the community he served, political repercussions be damned. There were already two people dead. How many more would it take before Case and his posse were willing to mount a mass effort at tracking down this creature?

"Listen," said Henry, "if you're willing to go out on this limb with me, I'm going to contact the media and tell them about finding the girl today. I'm going to tell them what she said about 'don't let it come back'. I'm going to tell them about what the hunter's son saw. I'm going to tell them about the footprints. I'm going to tell them about my encounter last month."

"What about your job Henry?" asked Wheeler, thinking of Henry's best interest.

"To hell with MacFarland. Two people have been killed now. I blame one of those deaths, at least in part, on that over financed bully. Cummings, that's my boss, is a good guy. He'll understand."

"Well, I agree. I think Sheriff Case and that county executive, what's his name, Finney? – have too much pressure on them based on their position in the community. If someone from the outside opens this thing up then it might make things easier for them in the long run." There was a pause on the line. "But it's going to take moral fortitude Henry. You're going to catch hell for this, that is, if anybody believes you enough to get any notoriety in the first place."

"Mr. Wheeler, you know I'm not looking for notoriety. Something's killing people in those woods and it's going to take a concerted effort to find it and stop it."

"Henry, through your encounter and now especially with finding this girl and seeing that body in the woods you've been drug into the emotional aspect of this case. But speaking strictly scientifically, would you be willing to kill this creature to prove it exists?" asked Wheeler, a deep air of introspection in his voice.

"Initially, no," said Henry, with a sigh. "But now, yes. I'd be willing to blow its brains out," he finished with great resolve.

"In light of what has happened I suppose I would too," agreed Wheeler. "I never thought I'd say that. I always imagined these creatures being peaceful, Old Man of the Woods type beings. But this episode has taught me that they are animals. But I still can't explain what has turned this one violent, assuming it is just one. Maybe it's that virus."

"Virus?" asked Henry.

"Remember? The one that's killing the deer. David Hix seems to think there is at least one recorded incident now of coyotes becoming unusually aggressive after catching the virus from a tainted deer carcass."

"That's right. You mentioned that a while back. I still don't understand how that can happen. I didn't think viruses jumped from one species to another like that."

"It's not likely but it is possible. Nature finds a way. David had some follicle on one of those hair samples he collected. DNA analysis should come back this week. It may tell us whether or not the creature that hair came from was infected with the virus. Of course, it may not tell us anything."

"There's so much we have to go on. It's seems a shame Sheriff Case feels compelled to hold back. I just don't know," said Henry, frustrated.

"Remember Henry, Sheriff Case is as much a social worker as a forensic scientist. He's got the trust of the people to think about. You and me, we only care about informed opinions based on the evidence. Go ahead and contact the media. I'm with you," said Wheeler in conspiratorial solidarity.

***

For the rest of the drive home Henry thought of ways he would break the news to a media outlet. He had already decided he would contact Iris Devonkamp with the story since she had covered the attack on Thurmond Raines for Channel 3 News. But would she believe him? There was only one way to find out.

Ms. Devonkamp,

My name is Henry Davidson. I am a land surveyor. I have recently been doing some work up on Yonah Ridge in Lytle County. I saw your report about the hunter being killed up there last week. Today I was up there hiking and found a girl who had been attacked last (Saturday) night. I also found the body of the man she was with. His head had been crushed on a rock. After bringing the girl out of the woods I went back to the scene with the sheriff and a couple of others to recover the body. I think these attacks were both caused by the same thing. I have evidence. But it's a wild story and I'm afraid Sheriff Case is afraid to tell it. Please contact me if you're interested in hearing more.

Sincerely,

Henry Davidson
(555) 555-5555

It was noon Monday when Iris Devonkamp returned to work and sat at her desk reading through emails. Her cameraman happened to be walking by just as she finished reading this evocative email from Henry Davidson. "Carl, Carl," she said, leaning around the edge of her cubicle catching him as he walked away.

"Hey Iris, happy Monday to you," said Carl, hoisting a cup of burnt black coffee in a toast.

"Carl, remember when we were up in Lytle County last week at that press conference?"

"Yeah, the one with the hunter who had been killed in the woods."

"Remember I said that there was something that the sheriff wasn't telling us?" she led.

"Yes, I remember. I was cold and wet in the rain but I do remember you saying that."

"Well I think I have an email here from somebody who wants to tell us what that something is!" she said, her eyes focused with the intensity of someone who truly lives there work, is exceptionally good at what they do, and sees their occupation and their identity as one and the same.

***

Music intro with anticipatory sevenths and fifths of synthesized sharp sounds. A camera brings the action to life then focuses in on an attractive woman, late forties, cropped black hair with thin strips of gray showing in it.

"Good evening and welcome to the Channel 3 Evening News at Six. Well, there's more disturbing news out of Lytle County. You may remember that last week a hunter was killed and authorities there weren't sure if the man was the victim of an animal attack or if he was possibly murdered. A week later now and it has happened again. Iris Devonkamp is in studio to tell us

more." The camera pans to Iris who is in studio standing in front of a large screen. Initially the screen shows a Google Earth image of middle Tennessee.

"Yes Demetria. This story happened very near to where the incident last week took place." As Iris said this she touched the screen and zoomed in to Yonah Ridge. "The area we're looking at is called Yonah Ridge. It is a heavily forested area, very remote. It is owned by the Springwater Paper Company. Even though it is technically private property, the area is popular with hunters and hikers alike. In this latest incident a man and a woman were out camping when something came into their camp, killing the man. The woman survived and was found yesterday morning by another hiker."

"Iris, has the woman who survived the attack been able to give the police any information?"

"Demetria, nothing of the investigation was mentioned in the press release and I haven't heard any word as to the condition of the woman who survived the attack. The Lytle County Sheriff's Department has not returned any of my calls or responded to any of my emails."

"Iris do you suspect they may be withholding sensitive information? You would think with two seemingly unexplained attacks in the same location the sheriff's department would be asking for any leads they could get and wanting to get the details of the story out to the public."

"Yes Demetria. I know it is dangerous to speculate, but there really haven't been many details released concerning either of these incidents."

***

At twenty minutes past seven Henry walked into the Java Gaia Coffee House and took a seat by the window. The night was cool but not cold, typical of the week of Thanksgiving. He wore a thick flannel shirt and a pair of dark khaki Carhartt pants. He had thought of dressing up to meet the attractive television news reporter but in his constantly over-thinking mind he thought that clean blue jeans and a shirt and sweater might be too much so he defaulted to his work clothes, which represented his identity. That's why he was wearing his muddy work boots and a heavy green cap.

Henry ordered a hot tea, Earl Grey, and sat down at a table by a window. He flipped through a field guide to wildflowers that had been left on the table buy a previous customer. At 7:32 Iris Deveonkamp walked in, dressed in the same clothes she had been wearing during the newscast just ninety minutes before. Being a television news personality, she knew Henry would spot her before she could even have a chance to guess which one of the dozen or so customers he was.

"Hi, Ms. Devonkamp," said Henry shyly from his table, half raising his hand, half standing up.

Iris smiled when she saw Henry. It's that blink of an eye when someone either makes you smile or cringe or feel nothing at all. The tension of anticipation left Iris' shoulders and she walked over to the table. "You must be Henry," she said, extending her hand.

"Yes, thanks for coming out Ms. Devonkamp," said Henry shaking her hand. "Could I get you a coffee or tea?" he offered.

"A hot tea would be nice. Its chilly out their tonight," she said, turning and looking at the menu behind the counter. "I'll have the ginger peach tea."

A couple of minutes later Henry came back with her tea and found Iris flipping through the field guide on the table. "That is a guide to cedar glades," said Henry. "It's a habitat unique to middle Tennessee."

"Yes, I see that," said Iris. "Some of these wildflowers are beautiful."

"Are you from around here?" asked Henry.

"No. I'm from Missouri. I went to college at Mizzou."

"Oh cool. I actually think there are some cedar glades in Missouri," Henry said, struggling with small talk. Iris smiled and looked down. "But you didn't come here to talk about rare plant habitats. Ms. Devonkamp-"

"You can call me Iris."

"Okay, Iris," said Henry, feeling a little awkward at the lack of formality. "As I mentioned in the email, I was out at Yonah Ridge yesterday morning with my neighbor's dog. We were just out enjoying the nice day. So, when I got back near the waterfall, I found this girl shivering and obviously scared. She was wrapped in a sleeping bag and huddled against a tree. I took her over to her camp site so she could get some clothes - she didn't have anything on when I found her - I saw the body of the man she was out there with. His head was crushed on a rock like he had been slammed down really hard."

"Did the girl say what had happened?" asked Iris.

"Not exactly. But when I first found her she kept saying, 'Don't let it come back.'," explained Henry.

"Did she ever say what *it* was?"

"No, she didn't," said Henry, looking down at the table.

"Do you have any idea what it might have been?" asked Iris, leaning in, her journalistic sense telling her she was about to hear a revelation that would turn this into a major story.

"Yes Ms. Devonkamp -Iris - I do," said Henry, looking her square in the eye. "I'm a land surveyor. Back in October me and a crew were out on Yonah Ridge doing a boundary survey for a developer who wants to buy that property from Springwater. One evening just before dusk I was up ahead of the crew setting our last traverse point for the day. Please excuse the surveying lingo, but I had to be doing something out there, right?" he said with a nervous

134

laugh. "Well anyway, I was chopping through some brush when I looked down a slope and I saw this thing standing there. At first, I thought it was a man but I inherently knew it wasn't. But it did have a human or apelike face, really like an orangutan or something. There was a horrible odor associated with this creature. Of course I freaked out. I mean, you know, just really lost it for a minute, terrified."

"So, you saw an ape in the woods, Bigfoot, if you will?" asked Iris, putting up her guard, the good energy between her and Henry beginning to shift.

"I, I promise that's what I saw," said Henry, holding up his hand as if giving an oath.

"Mr. Davidson, what exactly do you think I am supposed to do with a story like that?" asked Iris, slightly disgusted, feeling her time had been wasted by some fanboy who wanted to meet an attractive television reporter. This had happened to her before.

"Ms. Devonkamp there is no reason for you to believe me. But what about the little boy, the son of the deer hunter who was killed last week? Did you know he woke up in the hospital screaming about the monster that killed his father?" asked Henry, dramatically, defensively. "Of course, you wouldn't know that, hardly anyone does. But Sheriff Case knows it."

Iris looked at Henry. She was a good reader of people and she could see Henry genuinely believed what he was saying. "A scared little boy who saw his father violently killed and the delusional ranting of a girl with hypothermia. Is there any more evidence?"

Henry looked at Iris. His hypersensitivity caused him to detect a tone of sarcasm in her last question. "I'm sorry to have wasted your time Ms. Devonkamp." Henry stood up.

"Please Henry," Iris grabbed his wrist as he was about to walk away, "I do want to hear more. I just have to wrap my mind around what you're telling me. You have to realize this is outside the realm of stories I am used to reporting," said Iris, her blue eyes squinted with empathy. Henry stopped, smiled, and sat back down.

"Yes, there is more evidence." Henry pulled out his phone. "These prints were discovered near the sight of the attack on Thurmond Raines." Iris studied the photo, swiping her fingers across the screen to make the image larger. "Those are the tracks of an ape similar to a chimpanzee or orangutan."

"This is remarkable," said Iris. "Has the sheriff seen these?"

"He knows about all this stuff," said Henry. "There has been another sighting in the area since I had mine and there is an official police report which sounds like a sighting but it was reported as a prowler on a man's property. All of this has happened in the same area over the course of a month."

"So, the sheriff won't talk about this aspect of the two attacks because he thinks no one would believe him."

"Exactly," said Henry. "And remember I said I had done a boundary survey for that developer? Well, his name is Buddy MacFarland and he's pressuring the sheriff and county executive to keep these incidents as low profile as possible."

"But the sheriff's job is to solve the case," retorted Iris.

"His job is to serve and protect," countered Henry. "Lytle County is a very poor area. No jobs. There is real poverty there. It has a reputation as a meth capital because people have to do something to make some money. As it is, people have to drive a long way to factories and construction jobs in neighboring counties. This developer could bring in a lot of jobs and tax revenue to a depressed economy."

"I see," said Iris. "He's afraid if people found out this bizarre, apparently violent creature lived there that it would interfere with development prospects."

"That's right. And there is beautiful waterfall on that piece of land. That's what attracts hikers and campers. It has also attracted

136

the attention of the state and conservation groups who want to purchase the property and set it aside for preservation and low impact recreation like backpacking and hiking."

"I think I'm getting the picture," said Iris, totally taken in by the story at this point. "So, what do you want me to do?" she asked.

"I just wanted to let someone in the media know what's really going on," said Henry. "I understand this might put you in an awkward situation but two people have been killed. I think it's time the truth got out."

"You know pursuing this story will be a hard sell to my news director. In fact, I'd say it would be impossible," Iris frankly stated.

"I was afraid of that," said Henry, dejectedly.

"Unless," said Iris, slowly, her mouth pinched, her eyes cut to the side in thought. "What if I did a story about that waterfall and the conservation groups that want to protect it? Then I could even throw in a picture of those footprints and talk about the legend of an ape that lives there. That way we lay it all out there and let people put two and two together on their own."

"I think that sounds like a great idea," said Henry, excited. "Of course, MacFarland will have a fit. But to hell with him. Its time this story moves forward."

Chapter 22

Henry went home and opened a beer. He walked by his mandolin which hung on the wall and absent-mindedly strummed his thumb across the strings. He sat in a wooden rocking chair in the dim glow of a corner lamp and stared at a painting called "Lone Wolf in February" that hung on his wall. He had enjoyed his meeting with Iris. She was intelligent. She had listened to him, believed him. She was definitely easy on the eyes. But, like everyone else, she was more concerned about the perception of the story than the facts of it. Life is black and white for a single man not too concerned about a career. Do what you do day in and day out to get by. Maybe that's why Mr. Wheeler was the only one who really understood this situation and accepted it for what it was. Henry pulled out his phone and dialed Wheeler's number.

"Hello?" answered Wheeler.

"Mr. Wheeler, its Henry."

"Oh, good evening Henry. How did your meeting with the reporter go?"

"Okay, I guess. It took her a minute but I think she believed me."

"So, what about it? Is she going to report the story?"

"No. She doesn't think her boss will let her. Of course, I could say the same about mine. She said something about doing a story about the waterfall and the interest conservationists have in saving it. She feels like that would draw more attention to the area. But you know how MacFarland and Sheriff Case will react to that…" Henry's voice trailed off at the prospect.

"That story will go over like a fart in Sunday school," exclaimed Wheeler.

"Yeah. No *bueno* for my situation at work or our relationship with the sheriff."

"So, what are you going to do Henry?" asked Wheeler, with a warmth in his voice.

"I don't know. I'm a little disillusioned by everyone's ambivalence to the truth before their eyes. Two people have been killed. And nothing has been said to deter more people from going into those woods to potentially meet a similar fate."

"Henry, you're young and idealistic. You have a trade you're good at. Politics and the people that have to live and die by the opinions of others don't mean much to you. You know one man *can* make a difference. With social media and such, you can blow this story - this cover up everybody seems intent on – blow it wide

138

open. I'm not trying to pressure you. But if you were already thinking along those lines, I just want you to know that I think it would be alright," said Wheeler, with a note of the heroic in his voice.

"The idea has crossed my mind," confessed Henry. "Do you think I should ask people to come to Yonah Ridge and search for the creature?"

"You won't have to. Post the facts, post it on the CryptoWatch website, Facebook, Reddit, tweet it…get the word out there Henry. That's all you have to do."

"And then?"

"I suspect we'll figure that out once we see what kind of response we get. But if I can read the tea leaves like I think I can, Sheriff Case and that whole bunch running this investigation aren't going to have any choice but to go out and find this thing that killed those two men. And, likely as not, they'll have lots of help doing it!"

***

On Sunday, November 16th, a deer hunter was killed on Yonah Ridge in Lytle County, Tennessee. On Saturday, November 22nd, a hiker was killed less than a mile away at Virgin Falls. Eyewitnesses in both attacks described seeing a large, ape-like creature. On October 28th a forester out inspecting power lines described seeing a large, upright creature covered with hair in Bon Aqua, TN which is about four miles away from the site of the attacks. A week before that, while performing a boundary survey for a developer, I had an encounter with a large, perhaps six-and-a-half-foot tall hominid in a ravine on Yonah Ridge. The tracks in the photo below were discovered at the scene of the attack on the deer hunter. I believe there is an ape-like creature responsible for the death of two people. At least four people, including myself, have seen it.

Henry included a link to a map of the area then went live with the post. He stayed up till three o'clock in the morning researching and creating accounts on more than fifteen social media and networking web sites. He submitted his "press release" to local newspapers and television news stations. At the end of the night, feeling a little guilty for having offered the story to Iris Devonkamp but then running with it on his own, he sent her a quick email apology:

"Sorry for moving ahead with the story. I know you have a lot to lose. I don't. I just don't want anyone else to get hurt. Henry."

After sending the email Henry undressed and lay down on his bed. He was dog tired, both physically and emotionally. He wanted to sleep but was restless. It is discomfiting to be too tired to sleep, yearning only for the oblivion of dreams but haunted by the reality that will come tomorrow, today, sometime after the sunrise. Henry lay in bed feeling he had made a bold move, one of the handful of bold moves a person makes in his or her life, the sort of actions that decide what our lives will be like five or ten years down the road. For better or for worse, the future forever altered because of what we have chosen to do today.

Chapter 23

Buddy MacFarland scraped the razor across his face and nearly drew blood in his attempt to rip the whiskers from their foothold in his flesh. Dutifully clean shaven, he walked into his bedroom and slipped on a pair of charcoal grey flannel trousers, a powder blue, button-down Oxford shirt, and a tweed sports jacket. As he had done every day for longer than either of them bothered to remember, he walked through the kitchen and poured a cup of coffee from the pot his wife had dutifully started just before she herself walked downstairs to the laundry room to take her first nip of vodka of the day.

MacFarland was somewhere in the middle of his second sip of coffee when the breaking news flash came across the television screen. Murders in Lytle County, hairy monsters and apes on Yonah Ridge, information being withheld. A fine mist of coffee spewed from his mouth, staining the salmon colored carpet at his feet. His guts churned once then flipped before the full-blown outrage found an outlet in his now vacant mouth which couldn't quite keep up with the oaths of disbelief running through his racing mind. "What in the got-damned hellllll!" Once again, his mind giving orders faster than his arms and hands could react, he fumbled to pull the phone from his pocket. He soon recovered enough to dial Finney's direct line at the high school.

"Principal Finney, how may I help you," answered Finney in a congenial voice.

"Finney! Have you seen what is on the news?" snarled MacFarland.

"Oh, hi Buddy. No, I haven't seen anything. What is it?" asked Finney, still polite.

"Somebody's done it! They've gone and leaked out the news about those foot prints and what that kid said about an ape and what that girl kept babbling about. It's all over the news!" As MacFarland was going on about the breach, Finney's cell phone rang. Glancing at it he saw that it was Sheriff Case.

"Mr. MacFarland, Sheriff Case is calling on the other line. Let me call you right back." Not waiting for an acknowledgement from MacFarland, Finney hung up the phone and answered the call from Case. "Hello Wayne, I hear there's trouble."

"Big trouble," replied Case. "News is out about the footprints, the eyewitness reports, everything," said Case gravely.

"Yes, Buddy MacFarland called me on the landline just before you called."

"I imagine he's pretty torn up?" surmised Case.

"Well, let's just say I hope he has his nitroglycerine tablets handy," said Finney. "Any idea where the leak came from?"

"I'm not sure but I think it was likely either that Wheeler fella or that surveyor who found the girl. They were both pretty set on going out and looking for some sort of creature in the woods."

"Is there any damage control we can do? Or *need* to do?" asked Finney.

"All we can do is patrol the area," answered Case. "But with my staff, I don't see how it would be very effective. As you know there's only five of us and that's over a thousand acres with a handful of roads leading into it."

"Well, maybe we should just roll with it. Something *is* out there and it *has* killed two people. If we stage a big hunt maybe we'll get it," said Finney, being genuine, not thinking politically.

"Whoever leaked that information invited potentially dozens, hundreds, God knows how many people down here to hunt for it. Now I'm sure some of them are good, decent people who might even know how to handle a gun in the woods. But that many people who believe in Bigfoot, out there armed ready to shoot anything that is walking upright?" protested Case. "Even more

142

than becoming the laughing stock of the nation I'm just afraid somebody else is going to get hurt."

"So, what do you think we ought to do Wayne?" asked Finney, being realistic. "From what I've heard from you and MacFarland, this thing is going viral. And we have a limited staff to handle it."

"I'll call up the sheriffs in a couple of the surrounding counties. I'll ask them for backup on crowd control. I'll have to get David Hix with the TWRA involved. His crew can cite people for not having a hunting license and at least keep their weapons out of those woods."

"Well, that's a good start," agreed Finney.

"What will we tell the media?" asked Case. "They're going to start calling soon."

"I say we tell them the truth," said Finney, matter-of-factly. "The cat is out of the bag. And we did find the footprints. The eyewitnesses did talk about a big, hairy monster. We have something genuinely unexplained on our hands. And we owe it to the families of the victims to figure out what's out there."

"Yeah," whispered Case on the other end of the line, hesitation and resignation in his voice.

"Look Wayne, I'm going to be up for re-election next year too," said Finney, sensing Case's reluctance.

"Jim, I'm just worried about what will happen with MacFarland and the development and everything. People around here need those jobs. This community is dying. It's been dying for thirty years. There's no work here, twenty-five percent unemployment. We're known all over as the meth capitol of Tennessee. Well hell, what else are people going to do?" asked Case rhetorically, frustrated.

"I'm sorry Wayne. I feel the same way. I've spent fifteen years as principal watching the smart ones or the lucky ones graduate and get the hell out of Lytle County. Too many of the others leave school and go straight to one of your jail cells. But this is the reality of it. I recruited Mr. MacFarland the best I knew how, wanting to do something right for the people of Lytle County. But fate has stepped in, an act of God we could have never foreseen."

"Agreed," acknowledged Case. "Well, the other line has rung a couple of times since I've been talking with you. I'll keep you posted."

"Thanks Wayne," said Finney, then he went on philosophically, "As Theodore Roosevelt would say, 'we're entering our crowded hour'. We'll serve the best we can."

"That's right, whatever it takes," replied Case, sounding defeated.

Chapter 24

Iris Devonkamp awoke Wednesday morning and went out for a run around Centennial Park which was near her apartment. In her brown and white, tight-fitting wool sweater and skin tight running spandex, she made a striking site running past the assorted battle cannons and statues of railroad magnates. Had she been wearing a toga her aquiline nose and thick locks of dark hair would have poised her perfectly to join the goddesses that accompanied the gods and nude warriors and boys who acted out a scene of seemingly great excitement and agitation, frozen forever in the concrete and plaster that made up the frieze of the one hundred-and twenty-year-old replica of the original Parthenon.

After her run, Iris walked into her apartment and put a bagel in the toaster and set the teapot on the burner to heat up water. While waiting for the toaster to work its magic she picked up her phone and scrolled through messages and notifications. When she saw Henry's cryptic email her eyes narrowed and an unconsciously mouthed "Uh-oh" passed through her lips. She opened another email, this one from her news director:

Iris,

This is your story. Can you please come in early? We have to get someone on this. See link below....

Iris read through the post referenced in the link and smiled with excitement at a breaking story. She also smiled at the thought of Henry going it alone and doing what he thought was right. Iris recognized that there was something inherently good, something of the heroic in Henry. This story was proof of his courage and integrity.

Iris ate her breakfast and flipped through television stations. At the same time Buddy MacFarland was spitting coffee onto his salmon pink carpet, Iris was watching the same report of the "monster" of Yonah Ridge (as the reporter called it). As she finished her tea she replied to Henry's email.

You've really opened up a can of worms. I'll be in touch but keep me in the loop with any new developments.

Once she arrived at the station Iris quickly tried to calm her news director who was spinning in circles, spouting an over-caffeinated flurry of questions like, "How are you going to cover this? What are you going to do about this? Can you talk to this guy who posted this? Is he credible?"

Iris was able to settle him down with a suitably competent plan of action. First on her agenda was to call Sheriff Case's office and ask for a reply to the accusations that his department had been withholding information from the public. Next...well, let's see what Sheriff Case has to say first.

"Sheriff's Department, Deputy Chumley speaking," answered the other end of the line. Chris Chumley was wound up by the excitement of the morning and attempted to affect a deeper tone to his voice to show he was in a position of authority. But his bass notes came off a little strained. Another deputy had already warned him that if he kept it up he'd wind up with a sore throat.

"Yes, Deputy Chumley. This is Iris Devonkamp with Channel 3 News in Nashville. Does -"

"We are not talking to the press at this time," said Chumley, sounding like a robot that had been programmed to sing baritone.

"Yes, I see, but is there any plan for a press conference?"

"At this time Sheriff Case has said this is an ongoing investigation and we're not going to talk to the press," reiterated

146

Chumley, feeling his authority slip though it had yet to be challenged.

"But deputy, your department has got to acknowledge these seemingly wild allegations-"

"Look Ms. Devonkamp," said Chumley in his regular voice, well aware of who Iris Devonkamp was. "The sheriff is still trying to figure out what to do that's best for the community."

"I understand he doesn't want to be reactionary," said Iris, softening her tone.

"Uh yeah, he doesn't want to be reactionary," parroted Chumley, glad Iris had given him the right word but a word he would have never thought of on his own. "But, if I can have your number, I'll give you a call when he decides to say something," offered Chumley, not meaning to sound creepy but failing. Iris gave him her work number and her email address. She thanked Chumley and said, "Good-bye" then hung up and sat back a minute thinking of what to do next. She suddenly remembered from covering the Thurmond Raines attack that the county executive of Lytle County was also the high school principal. Iris dialed the school office, introduced herself, and asked to speak to Mr. Finney.

"I'm sorry but Mr. Finney is busy at the moment," said the secretary.

"Has he made any mention of addressing this news about," Iris paused for a quick moment, thinking on her feet, trying to come up with the least preposterous way to phrase the question. She deemed there was no good way and continued, "Uh, forgive me, but this news of ape sightings and possible attacks on humans?"

"Well, all that sounds a little far-fetched to me," said the secretary offering unsolicited commentary. "But Mr. Finney hasn't said anything about it this morning." Then the secretary realized who she was talking to. Iris had already introduced herself but facts are nothing until synapses connect and light bulbs go off translating the guttural utterances of human speech to relatable circumstances in our lives. The secretary half stated, half asked, "Oh you're that girl on the evening news with Demetria, aren't you?"

"Yes, I'm Iris Devonkamp."

The secretary's guard came down at the realization that she was talking with someone who she watched on television every weeknight. "Mr. Finney hasn't said anything to me yet but I think he's been talking with Sheriff Case this morning trying to figure what to do. One thing about it, they have to do something. This story is everywhere. My sister who lives in Des Moines just texted me about it! Let me buzz him and ask if I can put you through." The phone went silent for a moment as Iris waited, her fingers crossed that Finney would take her call. Then a click and the school secretary picked up again, "I'm sorry Mrs. Devonkamp but Mr. Finney said he isn't ready to talk with the media about the matter at this time."

"Well thank you," said Iris. "I'll be standing by." Iris hung up the phone, not sure where to go from there. All she could do was monitor the situation. Patience was not a virtue that Iris possessed or esteemed in others, but everyone in Lytle County was being closed lip. She would have to wait for them to make the first move.

Chapter 25

By early evening the story of an ape-like creature running around attacking people in the forests around Lytle County was garnering national, even international attention. Through the wonders of the Internet and instant communication Sheriff Case's office was being inundated with phone calls requesting information about encounters with the creature. A couple of news crews from alternative information sources had already rolled into town and when Case and Chumley stepped out of the office to go pick up some dinner they saw two campers and a news van with call letters neither of them recognized parked across the street.

Case and Chumley, whose throat was now sore from his affected phone voice, got into the Sheriff's Department SUV and drove down to the Ridgeline. As Case and the young deputy walked through the door the conversation stopped and all eyes turned to them. "Well Sheriff, looks like we've become famous, finally made the national news!" said one customer in a smart aleky tone. The crowd erupted in laughter.

"Yeah Wayne," began another older man who wore his foam truckers' hat at a jaunty angle, "I heard somebody say we was gonna get a reality TV show: *Bigfoot in My Backyard*!" The crowd roared with laughter.

At this point a tall man who had been at the counter drinking coffee stood up. "It ain't funny!" he said with conviction, "This isn't a laughing matter." The speaker was Kendall Raines. "My brother got killed out there just over a week ago. This isn't just about some crazy story on the Internet. This is about my brother. It's about his wife and little boy who have been left without a father." Everyone in the restaurant was quiet now. "It's about that man that got killed up there a couple of days ago." Raines paused and took a breath and slowly walked across the room looking Case in the eye. "Now Sheriff, if there's anything to what's been put out there for the world to see you owe it to us, who elected you, whose families depend on you and your department for protection, you owe it to us to be honest and let us know."

Case took off his hat and addressed Raines directly. "Kendall, I understand how you must feel having all this publicity come up around your brother's death-"

"Sheriff, I don't think you do know," interrupted Raines. "No more than I could know how your department feels right now under the gun with all this scrutiny. But you do know if what's been said is true or not. So, tell us Wayne. Tell us the truth." Raines body language relaxed as someone does when they've said what they have to say and rest on good faith that the other party will follow by doing the right thing.

"Yes, Kendall, it's true," said Case, looking at the floor, somewhat humiliated by being called out, but ready to come clean. An undercurrent of commentary buzzed through the diner. Then gesturing forward, hat in hand, and raising his voice, regaining his authority, Case went on, "I haven't seen the creature that has been described. Tracks were found near where your brother was killed. And Kendall, as you well know, Thurmond's son mentioned a hairy monster that attacked his father. The girl who was with the other victim described something similar." A heavy silence fell over the restaurant. "There have been two other sightings in the area," continued Case. "One was reported by a fella with the electric company who was out looking at power lines near Bon Aqua. The other by the surveyor, the one who put all this information out there."

"Why didn't he wait for you to tell everybody?" asked a voice from the audience.

"Oh, can't you see? The Sheriff and Jim Finney were too worried about re-election to blame a couple of murders on Bigfoot," replied another customer, sarcastically.

Addressing the last remark Case replied, "You're right Marty. I was also afraid such a revelation would blow that big development deal that Buddy MacFarland was planning on bringing to town."

"Well two people's dead now because of your ego," said Marty. A jolt of anger flushed on Case's face.

"Marty, nobody knew that thing was out there when Thurmond Raines was killed. And even after finding those tracks I was just trying to decide what was best for the town. So was Jim Finney. We need those jobs."

"Well what now Wayne?" asked Kendall Raines in his low baritone, satisfied with Case's answers, trusting the good intentions Case had espoused.

"Well, I've contacted Sheriff Spivey over in Van Buren County, letting him know that we may need some help with crowd control. I've got the TWRA willing to send in extra people to check for hunting licenses if people do start showing up with guns. Maybe that will keep a bunch of armed nut jobs out of the woods," Case paused, collected his thoughts, then went on, "other than that, I guess we'll have to wait and see what happens."

Chapter 26

Sunrise doesn't come early in late November in Tennessee. But as the gloom of a drizzly morning slowly brightened with the drab winter daylight, pick-up trucks and SUV's, some with out-of-state tags, lined the pocked blacktop of Sinking Creek Road where the old logging road opened on to it. Sheriff Case and his men along with Sheriff Spivey and his deputies from Van Buren County walked steadily up and down the line of trucks, briefly talking to the eager men assembled in small groups sipping coffee out of thermos cups. Above the low morning conversations of the men rose the bay of excited coon hounds, eager to be let out of the dog boxes that reverberated loudly in back of three of the trucks. Luke Sudderth who, along with being an EMS volunteer, was also president of the local 'coon hunting association. He had brought two prize winning Walker coonhounds from his kennel, dogs which, in the past, had worked well with the petulant pair of blueticks Bob Dugger had brought with him. Kendall Raines stood by the bed of Luke's truck, in quiet thought, letting one of the Walkers lick his hand. In another truck, parked just behind the other dogs, was a brindle mountain cur and a yellow black mouth cur. They belonged to another enthusiast of coonhound culture who had driven down from Ohio at Luke's invitation.

Wheeler's SUV was parked at the end of the line of trucks. He, along with Iris and Henry, leaned over the hood studying a topographic map of the area with the aid of Henry's headlamp. David Hix from TWRA stopped to greet Wheeler. He promised Iris he would give her an interview once the light got better. Eventually Sheriff Case made his way down to Wheeler and Henry.

"Good morning David, Mr. Wheeler, Mr. Davidson, Miss-" said Case, tipping his hat to Iris, his tone implying that he could not remember her name.

"Devonkamp, Iris Devonkamp," said Iris.

"That's right," said Case. "You had questions at the press conference about the attack on Thurmond Raines."

"Yes, Sheriff, and I'll have more today."

"Very well Ms. Devonkamp," replied Case. Then, looking at the others, "Well, I think we need to address the crowd before they get restless and head off into the woods on their own."

Sheriff Case called Sheriff Spivey on the walkie-talkie to let him know he was about to address the crowd and then he and the others walked across the road so they could see everyone. Case waved his hands in the air to get everyone's attention. "Well, I guess it's time we get started," said Case. "I know most of you are from around here but I've seen several cars with plates from out of county and out of state. I'm Sheriff Wayne Case and up here with me is Sheriff Spivey from Van Buren County. Us and our deputies are here to make sure this," Case paused, looking for the right word, then continued, "this hunt if you will, goes off in a safe and orderly fashion. As you probably know we've had two people killed in the past couple of weeks and there might be something in those woods behind you that did it. Now it's wet, it's slick, it's steep and with all this cloud cover it's not going to be very bright today so vision will be less than ideal. I don't care if we've killed a wild animal or discovered a new one at the end of the day. All I want is for everyone to go home tonight in one piece. To my left is David Hix with the TWRA. Before *anyone* goes into the woods Officer Hix and his officers will be checking hunting licenses. If you do not have a valid Tennessee hunting license don't even think about carrying a gun into those woods today." A groan went up from the crowd. Case continued, "With this many people the less guns we have out there the better."

"C'mon Sheriff, just turn us loose to go get that thang!" came an anonymous plea from the crowd.

"In good time," said Case with authority. "Now to my right is Henry Davidson. He's the reason you're all here. He posted about the sightings, the tracks, everything I wished he'd kept quiet about," said Case, looking over his shoulder at Henry. A low wave of laughter rumbled through the crowd. "Mr. Davidson and Mr. Wheeler here with the Tennessee Department of Environment and Conservation will be taking a crew into the woods about a mile from here as the crow flies, but it's about a ten- or fifteen-minute drive around some winding roads. Anyone who wants to follow them can do so. But first, everyone stand by your vehicle and Officer Hix and his men will come around to verify you have a hunting license."

During Sheriff Case's address to the hunting party Iris had walked around filming the crowd with a Go Pro camera. She had left a zoom recorder with Henry to get good audio of the sheriff's speech. After being turned away for not having a hunting license a couple of trucks started, the drivers angrily gunning their gas pedals and blinding everyone with their headlights in the morning gloom. They sped toward a country store down the road that sold the licenses as well as more coffee and country ham biscuits so that the frustrated hunters could return rejuvenated with even more caffeine.

The baying hounds raised the energy of the event to a fever pitch as their owners opened the doors of the dog boxes and the animals flailed in the beds of the trucks, waiting for the tailgates to drop. Once they did the four coon hounds and two curs came together loudly with a quick succession of growls, whimpers, and baring of teeth and then they were off, barking and baying up the steep slope ahead. The men followed behind, trekking up the mud of the logging road, talking low, laughing affably, enjoying the music of the hounds' melodious voices. Wanting to stay with Henry, but having the journalistic sense to know the dogs might be the most compelling visual of the day, Iris hesitantly followed the hunting party with the hounds into the woods. But just before she turned to go, she gave Henry a hug. As she released and stood back Henry looked at her, a little surprised, then he said, "Be safe," laying his hand on her shoulder.

"You too," she said. There was electricity in the air between them, almost as if they were the only two people present, each one's eyes peering deeply into the other's as if they were somehow physically connected and could not turn away. But then, as the last of the hunting party passed, Iris cinched down the hood of her parka and turned to walk with them.

Henry and Wheeler walked back to Wheeler's SUV. They consulted with four other hunters, all from out-of-state, all members of CryptoWatch, who would follow them around the ridge to the trail that led to the waterfall. Once an overview of the directions to the place had been given the hunters returned to their respective trucks and the three vehicles turned out onto the winding back country road. A soft mist covered Wheeler's windshield and an old-timey string band song played low from the stereo as Henry and Wheeler drove in silence, each alone with their thoughts, each sensing this was the calm before the storm, the coming cyclone through the wilderness of the human imagination, where terrors unmet take shape and premonitions of reality that has yet to pass offer uneasy glimpses of what might come.

Chapter 27

The hunters walked through the morning, fanned out across the ridge, lost in easy talk, taking a cue from the silent hounds ahead of them that there was nothing of interest stirring in the woods. By ten o'clock the mist and drizzle had subsided and, after such an early start, the thoughts of many were turning toward lunch. That is when the dogs lit on a trail, a cacophony of bays erupting across the ridge and echoing down through the hollows. At this sound thoughts of food subsided and everyone became re-energized with the thrill of the hunt. Hazarding the potential of being in the line-of-fire should anyone decide to shoot, Iris ran ahead of the group. Using the small camera, she was able to get shots of the men walking across the crest of the ridge, spread out in an uneven line, reminiscent of a civil war brigade advancing through wooded terrain under the threat of enemy fire. She ran further ahead, toward the sound of the dogs. All thought of danger had left her mind. Iris was caught up in the excitement of the hunt as well as the sheer joy she felt when she was documenting a riveting story.

After a few minutes the hounds stopped their pursuit, having converged on one small spot of the forest primeval, but their baying was even louder, more orgiastic and apocalyptic than before. "They've got it treed, whatever it is!" shouted Luke Sudderth excitedly.

"You reckon it's that monster?" asked Bob Dugger. "They don't sound like they're on a 'coon. I ain't never heard my dogs tree like that!"

"Yeah I don't know," said Sudderth. "Something's really got 'em wound up!"

Kendall Raines had been within earshot of the conversation. A deep resolve suddenly came over him and he tentatively fingered the grip of the pistol in his holster. He was flooded with the realization that he might soon be face to face with that, that *thing* that had killed his brother. His footsteps slowed a moment in quiet contemplation, then he recovered and moved ahead determinedly and rejoined the others.

Incorporating her skills as a trail runner, Iris moved much more quickly through the forest than the men. Crossing the shoulder of a shallow undulation in the terrain she found herself at the bank of a small creek. Across the creek, farther down the hillside, perhaps thirty yards away, she saw the hounds. They had a large ape-like creature backed up against a boulder the size of a Volkswagen Beetle. Iris's five sense took over and suddenly she was acutely attuned to every sensation happening around her. The horrendous odor of the creature became obvious on the cold, damp breeze that had caused her nose to run. The sharp baying of the coonhounds, the snarled savagery of the curs, the looseness of the leaf litter, and the softness of the sandy soil which shifted beneath her feet. And there was something else, something she could not describe, something beyond any of the five senses. A sheer energy that this was life in the balance, this was something great and unknown happening before her eyes, something we all understand intellectually, but a force so utterly unknown in any real sense to most of us, this sense of life and death and the rage of one living thing against another, the one force that has shaped every living creature on earth, the ability to survive through dominance or escape, the innate ability of an organism to destroy so in turn it can live to procreate. This universal truth filled the air with a blue energy that no sense of perception can identify as having a sound, smell, or color but every beating heart can feel as it happens. The sinusoidal wave of life and death, the electric current that drives the molecules which control our every action, thought, and emotion.

Iris froze by the creek, awaiting the men with guns. Hands shaking in fear, excitement, and all the other emotions that happen when our intellect and endocrine systems work together, Iris held the camera and was able to take video of the creature as it stood agitated, its back to the large boulder, roaring guttural bursts of rage. As some of the men came down the hill into full view of what was happening, they stopped in their tracks, momentarily paralyzed, blinking unbelievably at what they saw.

Through a combination of instinct and training, once the dogs sensed the presence of their human partners, they moved in for the attack. The yellow cur lunged in and quickly bit the creature on the ankle and, as the large ape leaned down to swat at it, the brindle cur grabbed the creature by the hand. Immune to the pain of the bite, the creature wrapped its hand around the dog's lower jaw, twisting it, picking the dog up off the ground, slinging it over its head through the trees toward Iris and the men. The hounds, whose job it is to hold an animal at bay rather than attack, crept back a step but never ceased the intensity of their baying. Stepping toward them, the creature hit one of the prize Walkers in the head with a crushing blow which caused the dog to crash skull to skull into the other Walker. It then picked up the stunned dog by the throat, shaking it violently before slinging it against the boulder, letting the dog drop into a $10,000 bag of fur and broken bones, the $2500 stud fee forever rendered defunct and uncollectable. The other hound staggered to its feet and wobbled off in a series of brain damaged snarls and whimpers toward the creek.

Moved by the destruction of his high-dollar hounds, Luke Sudderth screamed, "You sonofabitch!" and ran across the creek, firing wildly at the creature, never hitting it. On the far bank of the creek the injured hound, whose brain had been jarred beyond repair, snarled and lunged at Sudderth, his master, at which point, with tears in his eyes, Luke Sudderth turned the rifle toward his dog and shot it. By this time the creature had fled down the steep slope into the same deep holler where Henry had first encountered it. Luke Sudderth bent down in tears, stroking the fur of his beloved dog. The blueticks and the yellow cur had scattered into the forest in different directions. Iris and the men all stood in stunned silence by the creek. Bob Dugger walked up and lay his hand on Luke's shoulder. No one seemed very eager to chase after the creature.

Chapter 28

Wheeler pulled the SUV onto the wide shoulder and turned off the engine. He turned to Henry who had been quiet for most of the drive. "Well Henry, are you ready?"

"Yeah, I'm actually really excited," said Henry, smiling.

"Me too," said Wheeler. "I feel like today there is a good chance we're going to prove to the world that this creature exists. Years of myths, legends, hoaxes, a stigma attached to people who really have seen one. It could all be blown wide open today. With a picture, a body, a mass sighting." Wheeler took a sip of coffee and sighed contentedly. "And I'm just vain enough to be proud to be one of the people that brings the truth about these apes to the world."

"It's going to be pretty dangerous isn't it? If we see one?" asked Henry.

"Based on what's happened out here in the past couple of weeks, I'd say yes, it might be," said Wheeler.

"I hope she's okay," said Henry, looking through the misted windshield, staring off into the distance.

"Your girl?" asked Wheeler, referring to Iris. "I suspected there was a little something between the two of you," he said, giving Henry a good-natured punch on the shoulder. "She'll be fine. It's us I worry about, coming across the ridge right into the line of fire of that hunting party. But there's lots of trees in these woods. We'd have to be pretty unlucky for a stray bullet to hit us before smashing into a tree trunk first. But I say let's get on with it."

"Let's," said Henry, opening the door. The four other hunters, two armed with rifles, the other two with cameras, joined them as they began the trek out the narrow trail toward the waterfall. Rain dripped from the bare trees as the six men walked a few minutes in silence. They could hear the chorus of the hounds baying a half-mile away.

"Those dog's sure do sound pretty," said Wheeler. "My daddy kept redbones when I was a boy. I've followed that sound many a night, wearing a headlamp and carrying a shotgun."

"What did you do when you got the raccoon?" asked one of the men carrying a camera.

"We'd watch the dogs go at it. Sometimes it would find a way to escape and swim across the river," said Wheeler with a chuckle. "If it ever got to the river it would live to see another day."

"Did you ever eat the raccoons?" asked another hunter.

"My uncle and some other people would. But my daddy never wanted my mother to fix it at our house. We'd shoot it and let the dogs have it. We were poor enough that we'd feed it to the dogs, but we weren't so poor as to have to eat 'coon ourselves," said Wheeler, happy with the reminiscence.

After half an hour of walking Henry stopped the group by a hollow tree. "This is where I found the girl," said Henry rubbing the side of the tree. "Just over here about sixty feet away is where I found her boyfriend with his head smashed on a rock," he said, pointing to an opening in the trees.

The party grew somber as a passing surge of adrenaline and dread shot through their bodies at Henry's description of violent death. Sometimes on outings when we are confident in our position at the top of the food chain having the notion that we might encounter real danger gives us pause. It is the moment when you feel that fall in the pit of your stomach and a passing wave of weakness shoots through your arms and legs and you hope that you don't have the same reaction if the threat materializes.

After a moment's pause the six men walked around the side of the hill and stood before Virgin Falls which was flowing at low volume despite a week of misty, if not rainy weather. "That's beautiful," said one of the men who had driven down from Missouri. "I've never seen something like that. Comes out of a cave, falls, then just disappears into the ground," he declared, taking a picture with the DSLR camera he had brought to document the hunt.

"This waterfall is part of the reason we're here right now," said Wheeler. "This land is up for sale and after the deer hunter was killed that developer - what's his name, MacFarland? - didn't want much getting out about what happened to him. He knew the state and a group called Friends of the Cumberlands were already interested in buying this land and setting it aside as a state park or natural area. He didn't want any more people to know this waterfall was back here because he didn't want any public support for the establishment of that park."

"So, refresh me on the timeline again," said one of the other men from CryptoWatch. "When did they first suspect that something out of the ordinary killed that hunter?"

"Hell, they knew later that day. Those ape tracks were found very near the deer stand where Thurmond Raines was killed. And then later that night or the next morning his young son woke up from a nightmare and more or less told his momma that it was a large hairy creature that killed his daddy. As far as I'm concerned, that other boy that got killed out here last week was a death that could have been prevented," said Wheeler with disgust.

"Has there been any other run-ins with the creature besides those two attacks and the one posted on CryptoWatch?" asked the same man.

"Well, of course there was Henry's encounter. What's so interesting about that is Henry described seeing a dead deer in the woods the evening of his encounter. And the next morning that deer was gone," said Wheeler.

162

"What do you think killed the deer? Coyotes or something?"

"No, there were no marks on it," said Henry. "I assumed it was the EHD virus. It attacks deer and I saw several other deer over the summer that had died of seemingly natural causes, you know, no injuries."

"What's more," added Wheeler, "that virus has been known to make coyotes more aggressive, coming in and taking down calves and even yearling steers and having no fear of humans. David Hix with TWRA, who you met this morning, collected a hair sample out here after the attack on Raines. It wasn't a deer or bear or anything he could identify. It had some follicle left on it. The results came back Wednesday. It tested positive for that virus. I think we have a normally passive creature that some mutated strand of the EHD virus has made violent and aggressive toward humans."

The men walked around the waterfall, inspecting the cave up top but not venturing too far inside it. They walked around the side of the hill discussing new trends in cryptozoology. Wheeler lamented that no one had set up motion detecting cameras on Yonah Ridge. Then suddenly they heard the dogs baying frantically. Stopping abruptly and holding out his hand indicating the direction from which the sound was coming, Wheeler said, "I know that sound. They've got something treed. C'mon men, we need to get over there. I just hope we don't get hit by a stray bullet if they start shooting!"

Despite his sixty-some-odd years and increasing paunchiness, Wheeler moved across the steep slopes fairly deftly, albeit a bit cautiously. Henry on the other hand moved with speed and agility in the direction of the baying hounds, driven by his concern for Iris, which was heightened by the possibility that the creature may have been found. After fifteen minutes Henry and Wheeler's party came up the same side of the creek bank but from the opposite direction and stood next to the other men. The creature had already run off and Wheeler, Henry, and the others sensed the deep gloom and heaviness that hung over the rest of the hunting party. Iris ran to Henry and fell into his arms. She was a strong independent, professional woman so she could not understand the tears in her eyes. Henry held her close to him, burying his face in her hair, saying, "It's okay, it's okay."

Suddenly Henry felt a piercing glare aimed at him. He looked up and saw Sheriff Case staring at him. "Well Mr. Davidson, we've found your creature," said Case, his words dripping with contempt.

Henry looked around and saw the stunned, questioning faces, their eyes glazed over in disbelief. He saw Luke Sudderth sobbing, kneeling down next to one of his dead hounds. He felt Iris tremble in his arms. He squeezed her shoulder. "I, I don't want anybody to get hurt," said Henry, unsure of himself, uncertain if he had done the right thing by inviting the world into the domain of this strange, violent creature that haunted the dark woods of Yonah Ridge.

Suddenly Kendall Raines stepped forward. "Mr. Davidson you did the right thing. If somebody had been out here by themself, that may have been a person laying on the ground instead of dead dogs. I understand now what that thing did to my brother and I know it's left my nephew scarred for life. I don't know about the rest of you but I'm going after that goddamn thing and kill it. And if I don't find it today, I'll be back tomorrow and the next day and the next, however long it takes!"

A cheer of solidarity erupted from the hunting party, "um-huh" grunts of agreement mingled with amens, loud hooahs from a few Army vets, and one distinct rebel yell. The party crossed the creek and proceeded down the slope in the direction in which the creature had fled.

Chapter 29

The creature proceeded lightly, gracefully down the steep slope into the ravine. His every step was sure and there was no panic in his flight. But rage burned within his breast, a seething white-hot heat, unsure whether to flee or too turn back and attack. He had never seen so many of the others gathered together before. And a deep instinct told him that they had come after him. His hand ached where the dog had bit him. When he reached the creek at the bottom of the ravine, he pulled a large clump of moss from the rocky, moist bank and wrapped it around his hand. The cool, damp moss soothed the ache in the gaping wound while offering bactericidal properties, a fact which his collective unconscious had known from time immemorial. His brain, though highly developed, did not have the capacity for understanding things at the molecular level. His ability for abstract thought began and ended with pounding hickory nuts with rocks and using his uniquely shaped thumbs to grasp objects, while his rotating shoulders allowed him to throw them so as to exert his influence from a distance. This was something no other animal in the forest could do, except for the others. But they were weak. Yet despite their frail bodies he sensed they were tremendously threatening. Where he could throw a stick, the others could control thunder and hurl objects at him with a greater force than he ever knew existed. He could hear the rocks that came toward him when the others called forth the thunder, but he had never been hit by one. Another thing that made the others so threatening was that they controlled the other animals. The little wolves that lived with them, that they brought into the forest with them. The little wolves were threatening, making ghostly preternatural sounds that have never echoed through the hills and hollows of any forest where the others have not brought them first. Nothing in the collective conscious could tell him what these creatures were but he sensed they were an unnatural presence in the forest, just as the others, and that the two working together made a very dangerous alliance.

He walked down the creek, his feet making only the gentlest of soft sloshes as they carried him through the water. Using his good hand, he cupped the cool liquid into his mouth and ran his cut hand through the water with some force to push out any foreign matter that may have collected in the wound. After a few minutes he found the opening to his lair and carefully slipped through the tangled rhododendrons and birch roots. He crawled deep into his lair and in the pitch darkness lay down on the dry fragrant earth and closed his eyes in exhaustion.

Chapter 30

The hunting party moved slowly down the slope. In part because the earth here was pitched at a steep angle, but also because no one wanted to get too far ahead of the group. After seeing the dogs being thrown around like ragdolls, everyone was acutely aware of the strength and fury that raged within the beast they pursued. On the long route down the more experienced outdoorsmen among the group looked for clues to the path the creature might have taken. But they found no slide marks or disturbed places on the leafy forest floor. There were no noticeable branches that had been broken to reveal the flight path of this large, powerful creature. There was seemingly nothing to show that the creature had been there at all. It was almost as if it had vanished into thin air.

At the bottom of the ravine the hunting party came to a creek. Sheriff Case assessed the situation, trying to decide how to divide the group to cover the most ground. He sent half the men led by Sheriff Spivey and Deputy Chumley up the ridge on the far side of the creek. He would lead a crew straight down the creek, paralleling Sheriff Spivey's group as it patrolled the top of the ridge. Case held his group a few minutes, giving Sheriff Spivey time to lead his crew up the steep slope. Then they all took off together, a hunting party out for blood.

Most of those in Sheriff Case's group walked awkwardly along the steep creek bank, trying not to get their feet wet in the chill, late November air. A few of the men who wore waterproof boots sloshed loudly through the water. By now the bluetick hounds had returned and ran around the group, their noses to the ground. After twenty minutes of walking with no sign of the creature there began to be rumbles of discontent, second guessing and casting of doubt.

"I can't help but think it didn't go this way. It couldn't have. We ain't seen a trace of it," said one man with a stubble of red beard on his drawn face who had come in from out of town.

"Where could it have gone?" asked another smartly. "This holler only empties one way. And if it went up to the ridge then the other crew will find it."

"Well, I just want to make sure we're on the right track," said the stubbled man defensively. "I didn't come all this way just to walk up a creek in the wintertime and freeze my feet."

Wheeler had finally had enough of the complaining hunter. "Chances are we won't find it," he said matter-of-factly. "People have been living in these hills and hollers for two hundred years. Longer 'n that if you count the Indians. I'm frankly surprised the dogs treed it in the first place. I don't think anybody out here expected to find an ape. We've already got pictures and multiple witnesses. That will advance science."

"Well, I aim to advance it a whole lot more," said the stubbled man, brandishing his rifle over his head and cackling a laugh.

"Yes, I'll allow scientific discovery has historically been a blood sport," said Wheeler.

"I just hope it ain't any of our blood," said another man, halfway speaking to the group, but mostly muttering to himself.

"Alright," said Case, redirecting the conversation. "That's enough of that kind of talk." The group walked on for a moment more then something caught Wheeler's eye. Without speaking he caught Henry's arm and pointed to an opening in the river bank as the other men walked past it. Wheeler somewhat inelegantly sloshed into the water, crossing over to inspect the opening which was barely visible in a tangle of rhododendron and tree roots. Bending down, he saw something that grabbed his attention. Adjusting his glasses and leaning in closer, he saw a couple of long red hairs caught in the crotch of two branches. Shuffling back out of the bushes, he used Henry's shoulder to regain his footing and balance himself.

"Sheriff," called Wheeler to the group that had already passed. Case turned around, looking at Wheeler without saying anything. Wheeler held up his hand with the hairs between his thumb and index finger. "I believe I know where our creature is." Case walked back to Wheeler and inspected the hairs. "These are just like the hairs David Hix sent off to the lab." Case noticed the opening just past the tangled mat of branches.

"Do you think it's in there?" asked Case.

"It has to be somewhere," said Wheeler. "The question is who are you going to send in there to find out?"

"I doubt anyone will volunteer to go in there. I wouldn't, not after what we saw it do to the dogs," said Case, pausing for a minute, taking off his hat and wiping his brow while he thought. "If it went in, it will have to come out. We can post someone here to guard this opening," said Case, decisively.

At this point Henry spoke up. "Sheriff, we've already seen how aggressive this creature can be. Not to mention silent if it decides to sneak up on someone. I suggest we leave at least three people here."

"Would you like to be one of those people Mr. Davidson?" asked Case, sarcastically.

"No Sheriff. There's something up ahead I want to check out. Virgin Falls is just around the side of the hill from here. As you probably know, this creek is about to disappear into a sink. It comes out again at that cave above Virgin Falls. These are two entrances to an underground cave system. There are probably more. But we need to at least cover the two we've identified."

Case looked at Henry, as if taking stock of a brash young man coming of age, as he mulled over Henry's idea. "Okay Mr. Davidson. Luke, Jim, and you, you with the stubble. Stay here and guard this entrance. Go ahead and chop away that brush with your machetes. Don't let your guard down. Mr. Davidson is right. This ape moves real quiet and if it comes after you I doubt you'll ever know it's there."

"Sheriff," said Wheeler, raising his hand.

"Yes, Mr. Wheeler?" acknowledged Case.

"This creature has a tremendous odor to it. It's horrible like a mix of excrement and decay. Everyone I've ever interviewed that's had an encounter has said so. Even Henry here," said Wheeler gesturing at Henry who nodded in acknowledgement. "If you smell that, then watch out because it is close by."

"Okay, men, be careful and watch out for that odor like Mr. Wheeler said," admonished Case to the trio staying behind. "Everyone else follow Mr. Davidson."

***

Henry led the group down the creek. Iris walked with him, occasionally going ahead just a few feet to take establishing shots with the camera to document the terrain and the men in the party. She kept the zoom recorder running to get the sound of the water, the hushed sweep of footsteps walking through the forest, and the incidental conversation that revealed the hopes and fears, backgrounds and perceived futures of the men as they walked on in pursuit of their quarry. Henry watched her as she worked, impressed by her dedication, awed by her talent, taken in by her easy smile and welcoming eyes.

After they had walked perhaps a hundred yards the water of the creek abruptly diminished to a trickle then completely disappeared from the main channel leaving only scattered pools in weathered pockets in the rock and within another fifty feet the water was gone all together, leaving them to walk through a dry creek bed of sand and silt with water worn boulders scattered throughout.

"This is amazing," said Iris, being sure to film the suddenly dry landscape around them. "I've never seen anything like this."

"This is called a sink," said Wheeler. "The water has filtered down narrow crevices into an underground channel. It's one of the more dramatic features of karst geology."

"It just boggles the mind," said Iris still amazed. She stepped onto a patch of sand which shuddered like gelatin beneath her feet. Surprised by the quivering earth, Iris stepped back and quickly asked, "Are you sure this is safe?"

"It's probably safe," answered Wheeler. "Doesn't look like any trees or boulder have fallen in lately," he added with a smile.

"This is so unique," said Iris, dismissing her fears of being swallowed up by the hollow earth.

"Wait till you see Virgin Falls," said Henry. "It's unlike any waterfall you've ever seen before."

"I can't wait," said Iris with a smile. Henry smiled to, a little bashful at the outright flirtation that was happening in the midst of a hunting party which had just had three dogs killed by a large ape, a creature that until today most people in the group would have never believed existed.

Chapter 31

The three men left behind stood grunting and shuffling their feet in the leaf litter and muck where the water met the hillside at the bank of the creek. "Well, sheeit!" said the man with the red stubble on his face, as the group disappeared around a bend. He pulled a flask from his coat pocket and took a swig.

Luke Sudderth and Jim Gaither began chopping the rhododendron and roots away from the opening in the earth. Luke looked over and saw the out-of-towner take another pull from the flask. "You better not let Sheriff Case find you drinking out here," he admonished the man.

"Why?" asked the stubbled man, flatly. "It ain't against the law to drank in the woods."

"It's against the law to drink and carry firearms. Especially loaded ones. Particularly when you're out on a hunt," said Luke matter-of-factly.

"Well, I know how to handle 'em. I was in the army," said the man.

"Oh yeah? Me too," said Luke, in an attempt to establish some common ground. "I was in the 101st. Went to Afghanistan twice, in 2004 and 2007."

"I was in the armored division," said the stubbled man vaguely.

"Cool. When did you deploy?" asked Luke.

"I never did."

"How did you get around deployment? Everybody in the last fifteen years has been to Afghanistan or Iraq?" asked Luke.

"I got discharged. I went through boot camp and fucked up my knee then I went to A-school and they didn't want to pay to fix my knee, which they fucked up, so they kicked me out. Said I popped positive on a drug test."

"Had you smoked any weed or taken drugs?" asked Luke.

"Not enough for them to be able to tell. I took a couple of tokes off a joint one night at a party. Hell, I had to after the Army fucked up my knee. It was the only way I could deal with the pain. But it wasn't enough for them to be able to tell I'd done it. They just kicked me out so they wouldn't have to pay for my knee."

"Hmm, tough break," said Luke, dismissing the stubbled man as an idiot.

The stubbled man sat on the bank a few minutes chain smoking cigarettes as Luke and Jim finished clearing the brush. Then he spoke up, "Hey, don't ya'll wanna go in there and see if that motherfucker's in there? 'Specially you, after what it did to your dogs?"

"No. I'm good out here," said Luke. Jim nodded in agreement. "If it's in there and tries to come out then yeah, I'll blow its head off. But otherwise I'm content to hang out a few minutes."

"Well fuck it. I'm goin' stick my head in and see if I can't at least smell that motherfucker. That old man said they smell bad," said the stubbled man, taking a last swig from his flask. "I got a flashlight on my phone," he said, pulling a smart phone out of his pocket.

"Do you think that's a good idea?" asked Luke. "You saw what it did to my dogs. That thing isn't something to play with. And that flashlight on your phone ain't for shit."

"I'll be okay," said the stubbled man. "I ain't no pussy. You just watch my back like we was in the Army. I'm goin' try and find that motherfucker." As he said this the idiot man from out of town rose to his feet and walked across the creek to the cave. He knelt down and shimmied into the tight opening. Barely four feet into the narrow space, he found himself engulfed by the coolness and dampness of subterranean earth. "Got-damn its darker 'n hell in here," he loudly observed for the benefit of Luke and Jim who had

173

stayed outside. The man shuffled through the water a little farther into the opening, wincing as the cold water soaked his feet. "It's wetter 'n hell and I can't see nothin'." He turned and shuffled back to the opening, squeezing through to stand once again in the weak sunlight of the overcast day. "Hell, there ain't nothin' in there. Too wet. Nothin' could live in there. You orta go in and see for yourself."

"I'm good. Besides you didn't go very far back in there," said Luke, stating a fact.

"I went further 'n yer ass did!" said the stubbled man defensively. "Hell, you don't even act like somebody 'at was in the Army," said the stubbled man accusingly.

"Maybe not," said Luke. "But you do act like some shitbird that got kicked out." Luke stared straight into the stubbled man's eyes as he said this. There was an unspoken invitation in Luke's voice that even the stubbled idiot could recognize. He just turned away and sat in silence, chain smoking his cigarettes on the creek bank, throwing the butts into the water and watching them drift away. Luke and Jim talked among themselves about deer hunting, college football, and the scarcity of jobs. Common topics on a Saturday afternoon in Lytle County.

***

Far back in the cave the creature opened his eyes and stared into the darkness, incorporating other senses to examine the environment around him. He had heard the splashes of something entering his lair. From the smell and weak vocalizations, he knew it had been one of the others. They had never entered this end of his cave before. They had often come into the other end of his subterranean home, walking into the large cave above the waterfall. But most times they turned around before going very far. And only twice had anyone ever veered off the watery channel and climbed through the tight passageway above that led to his dry chamber where he had built his bed of dried moss and hemlock bows. But that was many years ago and they had never returned. This new intrusion by the others concerned him. Just as any animal experiences stress, the creature became agitated and uneasy, unable to settle back into a comfortable position. He tossed and turned restlessly on the mat. His hand ached where the dog had bit him.

The others had never come so close and there had never been so many of them. He sensed a great threat. When threatened he had always been able to take refuge in his underground lair. But now he knew it had been violated and he sensed that neither opening would be safe any longer. Just as fungal disease has disrupted the hibernation habits of bats and rattlesnakes, the virus was affecting his instincts too. His diseased brain told him to flee to the outer world. To fight, to destroy anything in his way. There was one more way out of the deep cavern. He hadn't used it in years but he would try it. He climbed down from the higher chamber where he had bedded down and scrambled back into the main channel where the creek flowed in total darkness. Using his sense of smell in association with drafts of air coming in from the three different openings, he walked hunched over to a large slide of hard packed mud. He began crawling his way up the slide. Up and up. Eventually he entered a low, tight chamber where he had to squeeze around an array of close-lying boulders that had tumbled into the earth from the eroded cliffs above. A little way further and the first rays of sunlight, filtered through dripping tree roots and reflected off pale yellow boulders, greeted his tired eyes. He emerged from the earth at the top of the ridge amid a copse of chestnut oaks and the strewn rocky remnants of a mountaintop, long eroded into the broken fragments that are but one waypoint on the rise and fall and continuing metamorphosis of all things that occupy an everchanging planet.

He could hear the strange voices of the others. They were nearby. But turning his head toward another ripple of sound he imagined he could hear another group of them, farther down the hillside. He turned up his nose and sniffed the air. He could smell the others and the strange little wolves they had brought into the woods with them. He listened to their sounds, smelled their strange scent, unlike anything else in the forest. He looked around at the large trees and a dim sadness passed over him. Something was changing. Though he could have never communicated it, his wrinkled brow and sad eyes were evidence that he knew he was being driven from his home. The bare trees stood as silent sentinel to his changing world but offered him no place to hide.

He was suddenly startled from his dim, melancholy musings by the others. Their voices louder, he could now hear the swish of their feet as they walked through the leaves. They were nearby and coming closer. He had to react. He had to survive. Turning around, motion through the trees caught his eye. He remained still and silent. They were walking right toward him. At that moment, in a flash in the periphery of his vision he saw it lunge at him. The yellow cur came tearing with a lightening fury across the rocky forest floor, blaring and yelping with barks, high pitched snarls, bared teeth, and snapping jaws. Just as the cur stopped in its tracks a couple of feet from him, the creature suddenly heard one of the others holler from a hundred feet away, "Oh shit, it's the monster. The dog's got it treed!"

"Get your guns up men! Shoot that sonofabitch!" yelled Sheriff Spivey. David Hix, who had only carried a side arm into the woods, watched on in scientific curiosity and, despite the violence the creature had wrought, a twinge of sadness. Here was something wild, something unknown, something that had only been speculated on as myth. Now it stood before him, likely to meet its end. As a wildlife biologist he had so many questions about how such a creature lived, but now he knew the only question he would be able to answer was how it had died.

The dog lunged in, grabbing the creature by the ankle, not letting go. The creature swung its leg, eventually shaking the berserk animal off. He then stooped down and hit the cur in the head with the back of his fist. As he did this, he heard the thunder the others controlled and felt the small, sulfur smelling rocks fly past him. He felt the fire as two hit him, one in the leg, another in his shoulder. He felt more sharp fire graze the side of his head and then he heard the thunder that had sent it. He reached back with his good hand and grabbed a stone he had seen in the periphery of his vision while fighting the dog. With all his strength he flung the stone at the others.

"Watch out boys, watch out! He's about to throw something-," admonished Sheriff Spivey until he was cut short by the crushing force of the stone crashing into his ribs, causing him to reel and fall to the ground, roiling in agony and gasping for breath. Deputy Chumley and another man ran in to help the injured sheriff while the others fired another disjointed volley at the creature. Using the confusion caused by the downed man, the creature screamed loudly, pushed a large boulder over the rim of the ridge, and began running down the slope, fleeing to his cave above the waterfall, a last desperate attempt to go home.

Chapter 32

The party led by Henry and Sheriff Case had finished their trek through the sinking creek and now stood around the entrance of the cave above Virgin Falls. Henry addressed the group, telling them his rationale for bringing them there. "We all saw where the creek went underground a couple of hundred yards back there," he said, loud enough so that he could be heard above the soft din of the falls, the level of which had receded in the past week due to the lack of significant rainfall. I'm pretty sure this cave is where it remerges, falls, and then goes underground again. The opening Mr. Wheeler found in the creek bank has to be a part of this same system. That means this cave leads to wherever the creature went, assuming he went into the cave we saw earlier. And based on the hairs on the underbrush, I'd say he did." Henry spoke with authority, collected, every word well-reasoned, flowing smoothly from his mind to its articulation in his steady voice. He was a man in his moment.

Several in the group who had not yet seen the falls, including Iris, stood in awe, transfixed by the veil of water, falling 110 feet only to disappear into the ground. "This is so amazing," said Iris, walking around, filming video and shooting photographs with her camera.

"It is remarkable," said Henry. "Ever since our meeting at Java Gaia I've been wanting to bring you here."

"I bet it's beautiful in the summer, when everything is lush and green," she said, smiling at Henry.

"I bet it is. I've only seen it in winter-" Henry was suddenly interrupted by the shrill bark of the cur coming from up on the ridge. Awakened from their falling water reveries, everyone in the party stiffened, coming to attention, listening, trying to detect from which direction the bark and subsequent howl came from and how far away it was. They heard the excited yells of the men in Sheriff Spivey's party coming from up on the ridge, followed closely by the loud crack of gunfire, volley after volley echoing off the amphitheater of the waterfall. In the loud confusion of the moment no one knew whether to take shelter from the erratic gunfire or to run up the ridge to join the action. When a couple of stray bullets whipped through the boughs above their heads and sank into the tree trunks with the thud of hot lead finding a home, everyone decided it was better to take cover.

From behind a large boulder Sheriff Case yelled as loud as he could toward the top of the ridge, "Stop shooting, we're down here! You're shooting into us!" He pulled a whistle from his pocket and started blowing it, which caused Wheeler, who was hunkered down next to him, to jump at the piercing shrillness. Just as Case blew the whistle everyone felt a rumble shudder across the earth and heard what sounded like a train crashing down the side of the hill, cracking and snapping trees along its path. It was the boulder the creature had rolled off the top of the hill. Iris, who had taken cover behind a massive old growth poplar, was filming the scene as it unfolded. Looking up she saw the large rock headed straight for the tree she was standing behind. Henry was twenty feet away behind a boulder. He too saw the rock rolling straight toward Iris. They looked at one other with fear in their eyes, then, as if reading one another's mind, Iris leapt with violent force toward Henry just as he reached out and grabbed her. The entire episode took less than four seconds but encapsulated an eternity in which the refrigerator-sized boulder smashed against the trunk of the poplar, splintering the tree with explosive force and jarring the boulder onto a new path in which it just missed the rock behind which Case and Wheeler took shelter. Then, in the blink of an eye, it rolled over a small hemlock, behind which one of the Bigfoot field researchers had ill-advisedly staked his life. The man was crushed in an instant. So too was his camera. As was Iris' camera, which she had dropped when leaping out of the boulder's path. Her photo documentation of the entire expedition was lost.

A cold jolt of shock, sadness, and fear ran through the group as they realized they had just witnessed the violent death a fellow human being. A beating heart forever stopped. But there was scarce time to dwell on the tragedy. Just as the boulder finally came to a rest beneath the waterfall, the woods were filled with an agonized scream as the wounded creature ran down the steep slope, trying to get to his refuge in the cave above the waterfall. As the creature ran toward them a couple of the men fired wildly from behind their cover of tree and rock. The creature kept coming, running fast, with abandon but with great control considering the steepness of the terrain. It ran within ten feet of Henry and Iris as they huddled together behind their rock. As the creature ran past the main line the group had formed some of the men turned to shoot at it. Kendall Raines fired his pistol three times in quick succession hitting the creature once in the back, causing it to stumble and cry out in agony.

By now some of the men from Sheriff Spivey's group had made it over halfway down the hillside in pursuit of the creature. They moved quickly but not nearly with the grace with which the creature had bounded down the steep terrain. Their path had brought them down the hillside on the opposite side of the creek from Case's group. Having the presence of mind to find a clean shot, a member of the group up the hillside leveled his deer rifle and fired a round directly into the creature's breast. The giant ape stopped and staggered, reeling from the shot, then fell to his knees at the top of the waterfall.

As the echo of the gunshot faded the forest was filled with a heavy silence. Everyone watched in anticipation, fear, and some even felt a twinge of sympathy as the creature struggled back to his feet. He stood unsteadily at first, his world slowing down with each weakening beat of his heart. Then, momentarily regaining his balance, he looked around through the bleeding red eyes of death at the others who stood gathered around him. He looked up into the cold gray winter sky where three turkey vultures rode air currents five hundred feet above. He sounded one last mighty roar, his last sounds in this life, the anguish of years of growing up and losing, surviving, and living. He stumbled a half step forward which precipitated another round of rifle fire from his pursuers. This final volley caused the creature to stagger backwards. Cold water flowing from the cave rushed around his feet.

The edge of the water fall was slick with algae where it was exposed to the sun. The creature's tough, leathery feet lost their grip and he tumbled over the precipice, crashing onto the time-worn rocks over a hundred feet below.

Perhaps it was the concussion of the tumbling boulder the creature had launched down the hillside. Or maybe it was the violent percussiveness of the gunfire. Perhaps it was the crash of the heavy body of the doomed creature. But whatever the cause, the earth trembled as if in anguish. As sands slip through the opening of an hour glass, the silt and fine gravel under the giant ape's lifeless body began to slide into the crevices below. Then, with a mighty rumble, a great chasm opened and Mother Earth received one of her last great mysteries back into her womb as rivulets of falling water streamed down a thousand small channels, like teardrops from the mourning forest. Then, as the weary hunters ventured forth to the edge of the waterfall to look at the creature's corpse lying crushed and broken, the surrounding basin collapsed, releasing boulders the size of small houses into the thirty foot deep chasm, raining down, crushing, burying, covering the broken creature, the earth taking back one of her own, leaving no trace for the human world of light and life to ever find again.

Standing in shocked silence, for a heavy moment no one said a word. Then suddenly the men erupted into triumphant cheers. But Case remained silent, staring down into the chasm, processing, wondering if he would ever come to terms with what he had just witnessed. Wheeler stood beside him, wrestling with similar thoughts. Case turned to him and shook his head. In a low voice, almost as if speaking to himself he asked, "What kind of a God could make such a beast?"

"One who allows a creature to live in fear and suffering," answered Wheeler.

"Do you think there are more of his kind out there?"

"I can only hope so," said Wheeler, wiping a tear from his eye.

Chapter 33

The morning had started out a cool forty-six degrees but by nine-thirty the late April sun had pushed the thermometer to fifty-five Fahrenheit degrees on a day forecast to hit the mid-seventies. The winter had been particularly cold and Nashville had experienced two major snow events (i.e. greater than one inch) and one ice storm followed by two straight weeks of below freezing temperatures. On many a cold night Henry and Iris had sat at Java Gaia drinking tea and talking about books, music, and the myriad other things lovers discuss when the conversation comes easy. Other nights they would cook dinner, following a theme - Italian, Mexican, meat-and-tater's - knocking back a bottle or two of wine in the process. They watched movies - science or travel documentaries, dramas based on historic events, occasionally a comedy when the world was too much with them. In other words, they spent the winter together and fell in love.

On this sunny Saturday at the end of April they awoke and had an easy breakfast of coffee and banana bread. While Henry went outside and checked the fluid levels in his truck (which had started to leak antifreeze), Iris packed two bottles of water, some thin sliced country ham *tenneschuito*, crackers, and some cubes of cantaloupe into a day pack. Then they were off, with the freedom of the road reflected in the easy smiles on their faces, the gentleness of a warm day and the promise of summer blowing on the soft breezes coming in through the open windows of the truck. They drove out of the Central Basin, onto the Highland Rim, then up and up around the steepness of winding roads that led to the sandstone tableland of the Cumberland Plateau. As they drove the stretch of highway paralleling the Calfkiller River the landscape altered time and last October and November seemed so recent, came to Henry's mind so vividly, that if time had been a malleable thing, he felt he could have reached out and touched it.

Just before turning off the highway onto the winding blacktop that led to Virgin Falls, Iris decided that they should pick up an extra bottle of water. Henry pulled into the oily parking lot of a convenience store where men stood around dusty pickup trucks, comfortably idling away the day. Henry and Iris walked inside and bought a large bottle of water and also a bag of deep-fried peanuts and a disposable camera that they had decided to pick up on a whim for the sake of nostalgia. As they were walking out of the store, they ran into Sheriff Case as he was walking through the door. "Sheriff," said Henry, extending his hand.

"Mr. Davidson," said Case, reservedly, shaking hands with Henry.

"I hope everything is going well," said Henry. "And that Sheriff Spivey has fully recovered," he added, referring to Spivey's broken ribs.

"He's doing pretty well I guess," said Case, with a reflexive smile. "We went crappie fishing together out on Center Hill Lake last week. He's still a little sore but that's to be expected."

"That's good to hear," said Henry.

"How's your buddy, Mr. Wheeler?" asked Case.

"He's doing well. In fact, he put in his papers just after the New Year and he'll be retiring in June. He plans to go out to Arizona and spend some time with his grandkids."

"That's good to hear," said Case, his manner a bit tense. He was holding his hat in his hands, running his fingers around the brim. The three of them stood there for a moment, in awkward silence; three people bound together by a life altering event, but really no more than acquaintances, unsure of the etiquette of going deeper than exchanging pleasantries, uncertain whether anyone could bare to speak of what had happened five months ago. Finally, Henry broke the silence.

"I'm sorry for the way things turned out. My boss told me MacFarland pulled out of the development. I know you needed those jobs."

"Yeah, this community needed them," said Case, then paused, as if collecting his thoughts. Then, looking from Henry to Iris, he continued speaking matter-of-factly, "Sometimes a place is just cursed. Once things start going downhill for a little town like ours, there's a tipping point where there's no turning back. Lytle County was in trouble a long time ago when the shirt factory shut down. Then Springwater moved the lumber mill to Mississippi. People - politicians, CEO's - making deals, lobbying for tax breaks, sending jobs out of state and overseas. People who don't know what work is, taking jobs away from the people who need them." Case took a deep breath, then looking past Iris and Henry, looking out on an uncertain horizon, continued, "I used to tell my son that life wasn't fair. But I always believed that with hard work you could overcome that and be successful. The best and brightest from around here still do that I suppose. They get the hell out of here. It doesn't do much for a town's identity when people have to leave it to make something of themselves."

Trying to inject some optimism, Henry replied, "But what about tourism Sheriff? Mr. Wheeler says it looks like a bill is going to be introduced in the state legislature to establish a park around Virgin Falls. That's got to help Lytle County in some way."

Case paused and then, with unexpected heat in his voice, he sneered, "It accounts for people like you and Ms. Devonkamp coming here and buying some snacks, maybe a tank of gas at the convenience store! That's not meaningful revenue to these people." Henry and Iris looked at him, taken aback. Case nervously shifted his weight, turning his shoulders, opening up the space between Henry, and Iris, and himself. "I'm sorry," said Case, looking down at his hat again. "That was uncalled for. It's just that I wanted to give the people here a little bit of hope. But sometimes that's just too much to ask for." Then, looking Henry and Iris in the eye, he said, "Henry, Ms. Devonkamp, it's been good seeing both of you again. I hope ya'll enjoy this beautiful day." With that Sheriff Case returned his hat to his head and walked inside.

***

When Iris and Henry arrived at the wide shoulder where the trail to Virgin Falls began, they found a Subaru from Murfreesboro and a Jeep from Chattanooga already parked there. They hefted their daypacks and were happy to stretch their legs as they started down the trail. The forest canopy above their heads was already lush with the tender new leaves of oak and hickory, sweetgum and buckeye, creating cathedral shafts of sunlight as the rays filtered through to the forest floor. They walked past flame azalea with its large orange blooms. May-apple, twinleaf, and bloodroot bloomed around them, the flowers already past their prime, ready to go to seed, the cycle of growth and decay, unfolding as flower petals in a brief blush of beauty, followed by the serious work of developing a seed that would hold the promise of a new generation.

As they rounded the hillside Virgin Falls appeared before them, a radiant glory of booming water and magnificent spray which caught the bright white sunlight that beamed down from overhead and recast it into prismatic rainbows, physics reframing reality into little miracles of beauty and inspiration. Henry put his arm around Iris' shoulder and she turned to him. They kissed, a long kiss. They walked around the amphitheater of the water fall.

They marveled at the Jack-in-the-Pulpit sprouting from the leaf litter and a late stand of dwarf crested iris which bloomed near the base of the rock where Iris and Henry had taken refuge on the day of the hunt. Henry knelt down, looking at the pretty, deep purple flowers with their rough beard and undulating petals. "Look, these are named after you," he said, smiling up at Iris. She knelt down beside him. Henry reached out and gently stroked one of the delicate petals and a sudden shudder ran through his body. He gasped and tears welled up filling his eyes suddenly, unexpectedly. He turned and leaned back against the rock, his hands over his face, crying. Iris sat next to him, sheltered him in her arms.

"It's okay Henry. It's okay. Everything is going to be okay," she said, a sympathetic tear in her eye as well.

"It's just so beautiful," said Henry, choking through tears. "I just, I wish I could show everyone how beautiful the world really is. The life all around us. How wonderful, how good." Iris sat with him without speaking, just rubbing his shoulder. "I'm sorry," said Henry. "I'm sorry they all died. I'm so sorry," he wept.

"It's okay," said Iris. "You didn't do anything wrong."

After a few quiet minutes Henry regained his composure, wiping the last tears from his eyes. "I guess being here again brought it all back," he said.

"It's good that we're back here," said Iris with compassion. "It helps us to heal." Henry held Iris' hand and they sat in silence, listening to the waterfall.

The fresh, warm breeze and the dancing sunbeams on the forest floor helped the intensity of emotion pass. "I'm getting a little hungry from that hike in," said Henry. "What d'ya say we find a scenic vista and eat some lunch?"

"Sounds like a plan," said Iris, mussing his hair with her hand as she stood up. They scrambled to the top of a large boulder, where they found a flat spot and spread out a blanket in the sun.

As lovers do, Henry and Iris lingered over a long lunch, bathing in the warmth of spring, lulled by the comforting shower of the falling water.

***

He blinked his eyes, squinting against the brightness. He ran his small, tender hands over the cool, smooth stones of the cave. He walked a few uncertain steps toward the light ahead. The wind carried the caw of a crow deep into the chamber, startling him and causing him to run back to the security of his mother's side. But after a reassuring stroke of her hand, he once again stepped away from her comforting bosom, though never out of sight of her protective eye. He walked a little farther toward the light. Through the round frame of the cave opening he could see a world of green, shimmering in a gentle breeze. He heard the melodic songs of birds drifting into the cave. Fragrances sweeter than anything he had ever known lingered on the cool breeze. For the first time, his young brain realized there was more to this world than he had ever imagined in fitful dreams. Beyond the dark corridor before him lay a bright world of sound and color, full of new discoveries to be explored. All it would take was the curiosity and courage to venture forth into the light.